Rachel H. Kester

AMISH CROSSROADS SERIES

Box Set 3: Books 9-12

D1414095

Copyright 2015 © Rachel H. Kester

All right reservèd

Amish Crossroads Series

A note for our readers...

You are going to read 4 episodes of the series Amish Crossroads.: books 9 to 12. This is the final boxset of this series.

If you enjoy these books, make sure to sign up here:

http://www.amishromanceseries.com/amish-crossroad/

for information about next releases, discount offers and FREE book from Rachel H. Kester and other great Amish Romance Series authors.

It's completely free, and never miss all the best in the incredible world of the Amish Romance Series.

Lastly, you will find in this book some uncommon words in italics, they are not English, but Amish. We will send to you a list with the translation of all the main Amish words as soon as you will be register to:

http://www.amishromanceseries.com/amish-crossroad/

We look forward to reading with you ;-) Sincerely Yours.

Table of Contents

A note for our readers...

Table of Contents

BOOK 9

Chapter 1

Chapter 2

Chapter 3

Chapter 4

Chapter 5

Chapter 6

Chapter 7

Chapter 8

Chapter 9

Chapter 10

BOOK 10

Chapter 1

Chapter 2

Chapter 3

Chapter 4

Chapter 5

Chapter 6

Chapter 7

Chapter 8

Chapter 9

Chapter 10

BOOK 11

Chapter 1

Chapter 2

Chapter 3

Chapter 4

Chapter 5

Chapter 6

Chapter 7

Chapter 8

Chapter 9

Chapter 10

BOOK 12

Chapter 1

Chapter 2

Chapter 3

Amish Crossroads Series

Chapter 4

Chapter 5

Chapter 6

Chapter 7

Chapter 8

Chapter 9

Chapter 10

END OF THIS SERIES

BOOK 9

Rachel H. Kester

This is a work of fiction. Names, characters, businesses, places, events and incidents are either the products of the author's imagination or used in a fictitious manner. Any resemblance to actual persons, living or dead, or actual events is purely coincidental.

Chapter 1

"I can't believe that this has happened, Bethany. Everything that we've schaffed for has gone up in smoke literally. We know who's responsible, but we don't know exactly who has taken over the mantle of responsibility for El Diablo. It's obviously somebody that has a gruge against us for bringing the mann down. I can only imagine what has happened to Mitchell. We've tried to contact him, but it's been almost useless."

"I know what you mean Jacob and we can't think like that. If Mitchell isn't around to tell us what's going on, then we are just going to have to assume that everything is perfectly fine. For the time being, we need to put up the united front. We need to help our people that have been affected by this catastrophe. We were making some real progress in lifting their spirits, but this latest turn of events had certainly gotten them thinking that life wasn't worth it anymore. I've tried to talk to them about the Bible; for the most part they are receptive, but I can still feel they don't know quite what to do." It's been a few days since we've discovered that the camp had been burned to the ground. The Deacon was beside himself and it took a lot of convincing to make him see that we couldn't just leave and abandon these people in their most trying times.

He was about to pack up and leave and take all the good wishes that we had brought with us with him. Jacob and I were steadfast and we told him that we would stay on and make sure that these people knew that we weren't going to just leave them in the lurch.

"I might be a mann, but I'm Amish mann with a backbone for hard schaffe. I don't mind telling you that I've been affected myself, Bethany. It's quite something to see something that you've built with your bare hands get destroyed in a matter of minutes. The ashes are my reminder that I will never give up in the face of overwhelming odds." For whatever reason, he had taken some of those ashes from the rubble. He was now carrying it in a small glass tube in his pocket. As he said, he needed that reminder to put things into perspective. Maybe these people needed us to finally talk about this.

We thought that if we showed them that we were working on their behalf that they would once again feel like things were turning around. Unfortunately, they saw this as a setback that we could never recover from.

"We've gathered you all here today, because we need to let you know that we're not giving up on you. You might think that we are leaving, but we've decided to stay and see this through to the end. If we can sacrifice being with our shtamm for a good cause, then you can roll up your sleeves with us and pick up that hammer and do what we taught you to do." A few of the men decided to pick up where they left off. "We just need to forget about all the good schaffe that we've done and just wipe it out of our minds. We need to start over. The only way that we can do that is with a fresh and new compassion to do the Lord's work.

"We thought that you were leaving. We saw the way that the Deacon took the news that everything that we had built was gone. We've never felt so low in our lives and yet you still persevere. You must know that it's possible that this could happen again."

"Henry, we know how you feel and we respect the fact that you are the spokesperson for the rest of your group. You're right, I'm the Deacon and I was quite hurt by what has happened. I tried to hide from it and I was almost willing to pick up stakes and let you find some another organization to give you the hand that you so rightfully deserve. You have Jacob and Bethany to thank for me staying. I don't think that I could do this without them. They showed me that they are full of love and that any bobli would be lucky to have them for parents." I had not thought about that, but now that

Frankie was in our life, I was willing to give motherhood a second try. I've never had a boy. I've always wondered what it would be like to see them grow up to be young men in the prime of their life.

"Now, Jacob and I are going over to that site and start all over again. Whoever wants to join us should feel free to do so. Just remember, there is a long schaffe days ahead. All we have to do is look up to know that He's looking down with a smile on his face. You feel it every time the sun strokes your cheek and every time the wind ruffles through the leaves. You feel it when you touch a little boy's hand and he looks up to you with this admiring expression on his face. It all comes from the mighty Lord above and we may have forgotten that. We will never lose the faith, no matter who stands against us." I was glad that Jacob was feeling the need to pound something with a hammer. That anger that everyone felt could be translated into the kind of schaffe that would be better than wallowing in self pity.

I waited on pins and needles, wondering if my words struck a chord and then suddenly everybody made this sigh of resignation. They picked themselves up from their bootstraps and they stood tall with a defiance that you could see. It was burning in their eyes. They were right with us. Seeing that we weren't going anywhere had given them the courage to stand up and be noticed.

Each one of them grabbed a hammer and followed us out into the hot noonday sun with no regard for what kind of devastation had now come to their doorstep.

Chapter 2

That whole day was spent sweating and putting our best foot forward. I felt my skin sticking to the brau frock that I was wearing. It was too hot for this kind of material. I was Amish and I wasn't about to change who I was. I would never take off a piece of clothing and expose my skin to the eyes of everyman. That would not be ladylike. I even wore my bonnet to keep the heat out of my eyes.

It felt like it was the hottest it had ever been in a long time. Those of the women in the group had been assigned to making cold drinks. It not only nourished our bodies, but it nourished our souls. It gave us hope for the future.

I was still thinking about Gabrielle and how she disappeared. It gave me a cold chill to thing that she had been captured and taken by whoever had filled the void of El Diablo.

"I know what you're thinking. We've been married long enough for me to see the writing on the wall. Gabrielle is a big girl and she's gone through hell. She's come through it in the end. Wherever she is, I'm sure that she's fighting every step of the way. You gave her that fire in her belly. You're going to have to trust that your influence is something that will get her through the most trying of times." I thought that I was the only one that had seen Gabrielle for who she was, but Jacob was right there with me. She was a damaged soul with a lot of regret in her heart. She just hid it well underneath animosity. I suppose it really didn't help any that we were partly responsible for her bruder's demise.

I pounded on that one nail and looked around at all the hard schaffe that we had done already. There were two houses with frames where there had been nothing, but the scarred remains of where those houses that had been recently built. We could've easily used a different spot, but we thought it was in the best interest to make people see that building again on the same area would be almost like a cathartic exercise. It would make them believe that the impossible was possible again.

"I've talked to some locals, Jacob and I can tell you that Mitchell is still hasn't been seen. There have been rumors, but they were reluctant to talk about them. I think that I might be able to squeeze some more information out of them, but it's going to come at a discreet time and place. I believe that my meetings down by the river will be exactly what is needed to loosen some tongues. These people are reluctant to trust anybody, especially after what happened. I can't blame them for that, because they've been through hell and like Gabrielle, they've walked out of it. It's just that they don't know which way to turn. They are only following our lead, because we won't be beaten down."

"We've almost done here for the day. I think we've done amazingly well. It still hurts me to know that this has happened. I guess in time, we'll see that everything happens for a reason. Right now that reason is schaffe to see. You're right and we all need to just forget about all the schaffe that we've done already. We need to concentrate on what we're doing right now. It's painful to look around and see in my mind's eye what I had done…gone just like that."

"It's not about what you've done, Jacob. It's about what you are doing right now." I felt infinitely better. I could still see that Jacob was not exactly back at 100%. I was trying to be a good wife, but at the same time I was also trying to keep everybody else from seeing the pain and the suffering all around.

I went down to the river and I sat with those people that came. I gave them the guidance of those words in the pages of the Bible.

"What you say makes a lot of sense, Bethany, but sometimes it's hard to hear what others are trying to say. We hear only the sizzling of the fire and the way that it crackled and brought everything to a standstill. We hear the crying children, as they realized that the homes that they were going to live in are gone forever. We sometimes can't take it anymore, but you and Jacob have been nothing but Godsends. With that in mind, I've got a responsibility and I can't keep it in any longer."

"Henry, you know that whatever you say here is confidential. I would never say anything to besmirch your name or make them feel like you can't be trusted."

"That's not the issue. I guess I just didn't see the point in getting your hopes up. After all, there is no real proof that he's still alive. Mitchell was supposedly on his way to stop a big shipment of something. What that is, is anybody's guess, but if I were to take a stab in the dark, I would say that it had something and do with weapons. After that, he all but vanished, except for sightings of him from unreliable sources that told of a man that I wouldn't even recognize any more."

"I'm going to need something more than just that, Henry. What do you mean that the sightings have told a different story?"

"They tell me that Mitchell is despondent, drinking himself into a stupor every night and then going and looking for a fight. He seems to be running from something or drowning something in the bottle. Somebody's going to have to do something to stop his self destructive behavior. Grant you, this is all hearsay, but in every rumor, there is a semblance of truth. I would say that he's in a bad place, but he still fights during the day to make his family and friends proud of him. It's at night where he loses himself and I think that a part of his soul has been terminally scarred by what he did."

"I don't know what to say, Henry."

Henry was one of Mitchell's men and he had taken the place of the one that had brought us here to see all of this transpire before our eyes. "I'm not even sure if I want to go back and be led by somebody like that. He is really going to need somebody to intervene on his behalf." I think that he was looking for me to do something, but I'd still not forgotten. I couldn't forgive the fact that he had killed that man in cold blood. I may have talked to him socially, but telling him that everything he did was right would be tantamount to me biting off my own tongue.

Chapter 3

I knew that we had brought Frankie here for a reason. I had seen something from him lately that concerned me greatly. He was vindictive, destructive to the point that he didn't care about anybody else's feelings. It was time that I finally sat down and told him what the purpose for bringing him here in the first place.

I found him skipping rocks across the pond. He had this sneer on his face that could only indicate that he was angry at the world and didn't care who knew about it. He had on the same clothes. He didn't even bother to take us up on the offer of wearing something that his mentor and friend hadn't given him.

"I don't see why I have to pick up a hammer and help these people. It's not like they've done anything for me in my life. I struggle for everything and then, for them to think that everything is going to be okay is preposterous. We all know that it's not and we hide from the fact that El Diablo, or whoever has taken his place has decided to wreck a terrible vengeance on all of us. I think the only thing that we can do is survive. The best way to do that is to forget about all of this humanitarian aid work. It only makes us a target. I for one will not stand there with a hammer and wait for that bullet to come screaming out of the sky."

"We've gotten more security and there are least three more of Mitchell's men that are coming here as we speak. They will look after us and make sure that this doesn't happen again. I just wish that you could see the look of elation on the kinner's faces when they see us working on their behalf. It makes me feel like we are doing something that is important and bigger than all of us combined. There is a spirit in the air. At first it was diminished by what has happened, but it has since returned tenfold. We bolstered their morale and given them a reason to get up in the morning. They don't have to think that everything is lost and neither do you." He was looking at me sternly and I thought I saw a loss that reminded me of another young man that was a Dr. that came here. He was also lost and we had given him hope and with that hope came a brother that he didn't even know we had.

"I've heard of all the things that you've done for these people. I see what kind of mark and legacy you are going to leave behind when you finally walk away from all this. I won't say that I'm not impressed, because you've done something here that most people couldn't even fathom to do. You gave these people hope, lifted them up when they were feeling low and you did it through sheer kindness and the words of the Bible ringing in the air."

"You must see that your friends are happier. They're wearing fresh clothes and maybe you should be to. It's finally time to get rid of those tattered rags. I know they keep you from thinking that things can be better. I'm here to tell you that I will make them better. I want you to pick up that hammer and you'll be surprised at how good you feel. It's an amazing feeling to do something for others. If you don't believe that, trust me, just pick up the hammer and you'll never be able to put it back down." His face was dirty. I knew that he wouldn't allow me to touch him and I wasn't about to do it by force.

That would be sending the wrong message. I walked out of there, hoping that my words sunk in, but having no idea if they did or not. It wasn't until I was back at one of the buildings but I finally saw him walk over with a hammer in his hand.

"I don't know what you told him, Bethany, but whatever it was has certainly done the trick." He cursed several times, as he smacked his finger a few times. I went over to him and I showed him how to properly set the nail. To use just the movement of his wrist to hammer it into place. It took a little bit of trial and error, but soon he was schaffing with the best of them.

He was even outshining a few of the men and it was putting this gleeful expression on his face that I had not seen before. It was called a smile.

"I only told him what he needed to hear. We gave him the courage to finally see that there was a better way than just death wherever he turned. It's nice to see him finally coming out of his shell, but I still feel like there is something wrong. Something weighs heavily on his mind and until he gets it all off his chest, there's not going to be any peace for him."

"I thought that I was the only one that noticed it, but I guess I was foolish enough to think that I had this special ability that you didn't. I was even thinking that it was just my imagination. With both of us on the same wavelength, I can only assume that he is trying to hide something from us. Perhaps he knows who has taken over the void. He's not willing to speak the man's name, in case it would incur the wrath of that said individual." He wiped his forehead with the back of his hand and then he stroked his beard like he was thinking very hard about what our next course of action would be.

I wanted to find the mann who did this and make them pay with some kind of tribunal. We could not do that and leave these people to fend for themselves. We needed to stand strong and confident and hope that somehow and someway that El Diablo's replacement would finally raise his ugly head. He'll them have it chopped off metaphorically speaking. We felt sort of like we were wasting our talents. I did feel sorry that Mitchell was going through his own personal hell. It was a crisis of conscience and it was something that would either destroy him or make him a better man in the long run

Chapter 4

"I sent out some feelers to see if they can find Gabrielle, but there has been no sign of her, Bethany. I know that this is not what you want to hear, but it appears that she has vanished from the face of the earth. If she's out there, then she's hiding and if she's hiding, then there's really no way that we're going to be able to find her. She is injured and she will need medical help. It's kinda funny, but you would think that clinics would have some kind of record about her condition. Nicholas was quite adamant that she has had other wounds." I really didn't like the sound of this. I was really worried about the condition of Gabrielle. She was a big girl and she might have been just licking her wounds and trying to get a handle on the fact that her bruder would never be seen again.

I think that she could take some solace in the fact that El Diablo would never see the light of day. I may not have agreed with Mitchell's way of doing things, but I could not deny that him stepping up had gotten the attention of everybody in the area. His name was synonymous with getting rid of the most evil man that had ever been introduced into the Haitian Society.

"I just don't get it. She seemed all for the fact that she was going to come to live with us. I just don't see how she could possibly disappear without somebody seeing something." I turned and saw the kinner playing and I suddenly began to wonder if maybe they saw something that others didn't. Little ones seem to blend into their surroundings and when you think that are not listening, they are all ears.

"I think that Henry has been very informative, Bethany. I think it's a good thing that Gabrielle wasn't found. She obviously doesn't want any part of this. I would never ask anybody to join our cause that didn't feel 100% behind it. How can she, because her bruder died and that is not something that we can just sweep underneath the rug."

"I'm apt to be in the same sentiment as your husband, Jacob. He does speak the truth and Gabrielle was quite affected by what happened to her brother. Nicholas has told me that there might be psychological issues. It had to come, as quite a shock to the system to see her brother killed like that. We may have thought that she was perfectly fine, but underneath it, she might have been just a cauldron ready to boil over." Henry and Jacob were trying to make me see that it was a lost cause to try to find Gabrielle. I didn't see it that way. I had become quite close to her and thought that I was finding a kindred spirit.

If she really was taking some time for herself, then I could understand a little bit of something like that. It'd been three days and still no visible sign of her anywhere. I wanted to scream her name, until I was hoarse, but I knew that it would do no good. These lands were full of all sorts of dangerous elements. If she had gotten lost, then there would be no way to find her. The animals would take care of that; it was the natural order of things.

"I still have one other avenue that I can pursue." Jacob followed me over to the little one, who were talking to a few couples from other Haitian villages that had come to see if they could be suitable families. Everybody was having a great time and I could see the look of hope spread from not only the children, but to their perspective parents as well.

"I'm glad that everyone is having a good time, but I would like to speak to all of you about a serious matter. If you don't mind, if you can just sit in a circle, I would like to introduce you to these people that you've been having fun with. First though, I would like to ask all of you if any of you had seen what happened to Gabrielle." At the sound of her name, everybody became still and you could literally hear a pin drop.

"You're not going to be in any trouble. I just want to know that she's OK." Nobody was talking and it was like they had this pact and everybody was looking at each other and trying to decide if one of them was going to go against it.

"I guess it doesn't really matter. The thing that matters the most is that you have new families." I went about to introduce the couples. It was almost like a light went off over the kinner's heads. They played up the fact that they were cute and before long, every one of them had a place that they could call home. They even had an open invitation to come back to pick up a hammer. Frankie was the only one left and he didn't seem at all interested in what these people had to say. Ever since I had my little talk, he had become quite the hard schaffer. He was the first one to grab a hammer in the morning with Jacob leading the charge.

I don't think he wanted anybody, but myself and Jacob. He didn't want to be treated like any other child. He was older; more experienced and had a wisdom that went beyond his age.

Jacob and I were holding hands and looking at the happy expressions on everybody's faces. It made us proud to know that we had made this difference, even though it came with great sacrifices and loss that everybody would feel for some time to come.

"Bethany, I would say that Frankie is our responsibility. I know that this doesn't come as a great shock to you. You yourself have been doting on him hand and foot. You don't coddle the boy, but you do make him feel like he's loved and wanted. It's the reason why he doesn't want to be without us. We're going to have to treat him like an equal. We'll raise him in the Amish lifestyle and I think that our morality will rub off on him." I like that things were looking up, but I was afraid that darkness was soon to follow.

Chapter 5

The next morning, I found Jacob standing by a tree and breathing deeply and holding on to his knees for support. I put my hand on his shoulder. He looked back to see my smiling face. I was wearing a weiss dress all the way down to my ankles. There was no exposed skin and I was wearing my bonnet and holding on to it, as a light breeze had picked up.

"I knew that something was bothering you. You've been putting up this front for way too long. You've obviously been affected by all of this. I can't blame you for that. It was you that led everybody by the hand. It was you that showed that through hard schaffe comes a certain degree of pride in your work. You lost all of that and I'm sorry for that. We really can't dwell on something that can't be changed." I was trying to give him the right words that would convey to him just how important it was for him to stand up and not fall down in the face of something so horrific.

Most men would have curled down if they were in his position, but he had found a way to look at it from a different way.

"That's easier said than done, Bethany. You're right and I might've been the most affected by all of this. It was after all my doing to get people to pick up a hammer. I taught them everything that they knew and to see it all destroyed had placed a dark shadow over my heart. It's not as bad as you might think. It could've been worse without you by my side."

"You've forgotten that there is one other person that has always been by your side, Jacob. Let me remind you of the mann himself. I'd picked out the Bible from underneath my dress and I presented it to him with the gleaming cross on the side. He smiled, kind of sheepishly, but at least he was giving into his desire to find his faith again. "Gott has always been with you. His words have always been a growing reminder that things can get bad, but then they can get better. We all have tests and tribulations to go through and it's what we do with them that makes us who we are. You can't say that what you've done the last three days hasn't shown you that destruction can be rebuilt. It doesn't matter how many times they push you down. It matters how many times you stand up and not allow them to keep you down."

He opened the Bible to a certain phrase and he would mumble it underneath his breath over and over again. I wasn't sure what it was, but this was his cross to bear.

All I could do was be there for him and give him my undying love. The best medicine was the words that he was speaking from the very pages that had been passed down from generation to generation.

"You always seem to have the right thing to say to just about everybody and that includes me, Bethany. I can't thank you enough for that. You've never been more clear headed when all of this transpired. I hope you know that your dedication and the way that you speak those words so eloquently has certainly done this heart proud." He took me into his arms and he kissed me lightly.

I pushed away from him. I wasn't really comfortable with public displays of affection. He had gotten carried away and he looked around to make sure that we hadn't been noticed. I was thankful that our little show had not been seen by anybody.

"What we need to do, Jacob is to put all this behind us. We need to do what we've been preaching and wipe it clean from our memories, so that it doesn't have a hold on us. We can't allow this one experience to sully all the good schaffe that we've done up to this point. It doesn't matter that they destroyed what we built with our own two hands. It does matter if we allow them to stop us from schaffing these miracles in the name of Gott himself."

"I now see that we've never been closer, Bethany. You saw something that told you that I was in distress and you were able to show me the light one more time. I will never get over the fact that you can see me like that. Nobody else has been able to and I guess I don't see myself as a lost cause. I see myself as a cause that is worth a few sacrifices. This little setback is only a part of the story. The rest of that story has not been written yet and it's time for us to get back what has been taken." He held onto the Bible with a death grip. I could see how much he wanted to change that frown to a smile.

Frankie was the biggest surprise. Since he had taken us as his Guardians, I had begun to see a little boy turn to a mann. Frankie showed more guts and determination than anybody. Each time that he stood toe to toe with me and Jacob, it was like we were our own unique shtamm. I think with him by my side and Jacob's, he had given us a new spirit of hope that was seen in not only our eyes, but in those that had decided to wash all of this ugliness away from their souls.

I was only going to stay for one more round of volunteering. Seeing all of this had put me into a frame of mind that thought it would've been worse if we weren't around to make people see that life was worth everything that you put into it.

Chapter 6

The courage to stand up to true evil was almost too much for most people to bear. Our little group had taken his defiance and his need to put people down and made something beautiful from it.

I was busy hammering a nail and making sure that Frankie was not hurting himself. I needn't have worried, because he had already gone through the pain of hitting his finger too many times to count. He was now quite proficient. I was quite amazed that he could take up carpentry with such ease. It almost like he was destined to be with us. Then I saw Jacob talking to Henry and they seemed to be in some very serious discussions.

"…need Bethany to show us that not all of our good work was for nothing. With Mitchell's constant decline and the fact that he disappears for hours on end, it's a wonder that we are able to stand up to the forces of El Diablo."

"What is this that I hear about El Diablo? I thought that we got rid of him and his men."

"Apparently, there is a faction of El Diablo's men that are still making waves in the villages. Thankfully, Mitchell's men are able to keep things relatively calm. For the most part, El Diablo's men are flying without a leader. There's obviously somebody pulling the strings, but whoever it is does not have the same kind of power that El Diablo had over his men. A lot of them have become bitter and restless, leaving only a few to pick up where the others have left off. Henry was telling me about a few men that have gone on notice to say that they want to change their ways."

"That's admirable that they would want to do that, especially after what they've done to the good people of these villages. I'm not averse to allowing them to find some kind of penance. They're going to have to realize that their word is never going to be enough for anybody." It was nice to see that what we had done was not just one sided. Those men that wanted a second chance would have to come forward and formally denounce everything that they've done. I told this to Henry. He got this absentminded look on his face that told me that not a lot of people were going to jump at the chance to become better than what they were. He was going to send out word. We were just going to have to wait to see who among them would see that there was a better way.

"I'll do what I can, but I can't promise anything. That's a pretty tall order for them and it's not a pill that they really going to swallow." If only one would rise to the occasion, I would be so happy that I would sing the praises of the Lord from the highest mountaintop.

Those that were at the makeshift gate with their hand out, suddenly disbursed, leaving behind one man that wasn't so sure that he wanted to walk away.

"My name is Jonathan Wexler and I'm ashamed to say that I was a part of El Diablo's reign of terror. It was not my intention to become some kind of monster. I thought that he was a good man and it wasn't until later that I began to see the truth. I was afraid to say anything and I guess I was a coward. I'm not afraid to admit it. I just want a second chance to prove myself and I'll do anything." Jacob was the first one to come forward with a hammer in hand. At first Jonathon cringed in fear, but then Jacob smiled and placed the hammer in his hand.

"I think that trust is something that is earned. The only way that you're going to earn it is if you do it out in the open for everybody to see. You can't hide from everybody's scrutinizing eyes. You're going to have to deal with the fact that you caused them misery. This is your time to do penance and to wipe that slate clean once and for all. It's not going to be easy and they're not going to welcome you into the fold with open arms.

Most of them will be standoffish, give you dirty looks and probably call you every name in the book. You need to turn the other cheek, give them a glowing smile and not pick a fight the entire time that you are here."

"I think that what my husband, Jacob is telling you is that you have a hard road ahead of you. There are a lot of fences that need mending and you're going to have to stand there and take the verbal abuse as much as possible. You can walk away, but you can't raise your hand in anger. If you do so, then we will know that you're not serious. We will send you away with your soul still scarred from what you've done."

The second part of that scenario was Jacob, I and the Deacon sitting down with Jonathan and giving him the third degree. It was not easy to hear his sins made in the name of El Diablo. It was not something that I wanted to hear, but it was necessary to unburden himself and let that weight on his shoulders finally fall to the ground where it belonged. It was a long arduous regaling of his story. For the most part I felt sorry for him. He had gotten in over his head. He thought he was doing good and it had turned into something ugly in a hurry. He believed in the rule of law and El Diablo had played on his sympathy for the underdog. He was soon to realize that El Diablo's true purpose was to make a lot of money on the backs of people that were already scared.

Chapter 7

"I've never wanted any of this and I hope that you can believe that I would never consciously hurt anybody. I have a son back in the State's named Johnny and I would never want to give him any reason to hate me." It was time that we finally got down to what we had come here for. He had seen El Diablo up close and personal and it was not the stretch of the imagination to believe that he had seen El Diablo's face.

"I can understand that you want to do what's right by your son. You want to make a good example out of yourself. What you need to do now is to tell us if this is the man that you called the leader or El Diablo for that matter." I was reluctant to say the name, because it was blasphemous and the devil was in the heart of every mann woman and child. He influenced the decisions that we made each day. If we were true of heart, those decisions would be the right one. If we weren't, then evil would penetrate our soul and take up permanent residence.

I took out the photograph that I'd taken of El Diablos body and I placed it in front of Jonathan. His clean shaven face took on a concentrated tone. I looked into his eyes to see if he was trying to undermine everything that we were doing. It could be that we had just let in our own personal Trojan horse. We had to make sure that he could be trusted.

"Is this the man that you took orders from? Was he the one that made you do those things in the name of something that was good? It's too bad that you don't have the chance to confront the mann that put you through all of this. Unfortunately, that decision was out of my hands. I want you to take a good look at that photograph and tell me that he is the man that you've been taking orders from." I saw that he was looking at it and then he picked up the photograph and brought it close to his face. His eyes were wide, but I did not see the kind of recognition that would come from the discovery that he was looking at pure evil itself.

"I'm sorry, but I just don't know. I didn't really see his face. There were times that he would lower his guard and take off the mask. It was always with his back towards me and I'm not just saying that to make you think that I'm on the level. I'm saying that because it's the truth. On my child's life, I will say unequivocally that I've not seen his face. There is something strange; that photograph that you showed me doesn't feel right. I can't explain it and there is something definitely different about the way that this man's eyes look at me from the photograph. The person that looked at me before was cold and ice penetrated his very soul. His voice was husky, but I felt like he was trying to hide that from us as well." He was standing there pacing back and forth and he still had the photograph. He was taping it against his forehead every so often.

"I understand this might be difficult for you to say anything negative about the man that you did work for. I'm hoping that you are not lying to us, but I don't sense that there is any kind of untruth coming from your lips. I'm a pretty good judge of character and I would say that you're being on the level, albeit a little standoffish for my liking."

"Bethany, he's doing everything he can to make things right and we need to give him a chance. I know this is not going to be easy for anybody and I suspect that there is going to be a lot of hurt feelings. Not everybody is going to understand that he's here with us and the rumors are going to spread like wildfire." The Deacon was only trying to be the voice of reason and I could see that not even he could trust everything that was coming out of Jonathan's mouth.

"I told you everything that I can and I'm ready to do what I have to to make up for everything that I've done. I should've walked away, but I was afraid that I would find myself on the receiving end of the wrath of El

Diablo himself. It was cowardly and wrong and I was just afraid that I would lose my life and my little boy would have to grow up without a father. That's not an excuse, it's just a fact and the way that I felt at the time. Trust me, my boy needs extra care and he can be quite a handful with someone that doesn't really know how he is at any given time." There was no reason to despair and we took him out to the site of those two frames that we had recently put up.

It was still early in the afternoon and Frankie was the first one to look over and come to greet a man that he had seen firsthand. He kicked him in the shin. He was doubled over and Frankie slapped him across the face, so hard that you could hear the collective gasp of the crowd. He then walked back over to pick up his hammer and went right back to work. That kid was something else. He really didn't mince words or try to hide his feelings in any way.

Jonathan was a good man underneath it all, or at least that was the perception that I was getting from him. There's no denying that he had a son. He had shown us photographs to prove to us that he wasn't just telling a story for the sake of getting our sympathy. I wanted to believe that people could change, but I'd seen many times that that wasn't the case. I was hoping that Jonathan would be the exception to that rule and as he started to hammer a nail, I began to wonder maybe we had found a cause that was worthy.

Chapter 8

"I know that this is something that is not going to be received kindly, but we have no choice to give this mann the benefit of the doubt. He claims that he was tricked into working for El Diablo and that he has never wanted to hurt anybody. I know that this will come as a shock to all of you, but together with my husband we have decided that this mann deserves the chance to prove himself to all of us. It's the reason why we gave him a hammer and is the reason why he is standing there working underneath the sun with all of us." I've no doubt that Jonathan could hear everything that was being said, but he was trying to remain as elusive as possible.

"I don't like it and I know that the others are not going to say anything, but they don't like it either. We trust that you know what you're doing and we hope for your sake that this doesn't come back and bite you. He could be a plant and this could be a trap that will lull us into a false sense of security."

"Jacob and I have taken everything into consideration and we feel that he is warranted the chance to redeem himself. Besides, there is a contingent of Mitchell's men outside of the makeshift gate. They'll make sure that nobody gets close without their personal OK. That's the best that we can do and we can only do so much. We have to take everything in faith. We all know that our faith has been shaken, but it has not been broken and nothing will ever break it." I did notice that Frankie was trying to stay away from Jonathan as much as possible.

"Like we said, we will work with him, but that doesn't mean that we have to like him. He's just going to have to get used to people muttering underneath their breath and giving him dirty looks the entire time that he stands here with us." I could understand where they were coming from. I could also see that they were willing to open up their hearts towards a mann that could possibly be the devil in disguise.

"That's all we can ask for. My wife, Bethany and I really do appreciate the way that you've decided to let him find a way to make it up to all of us. He needs to purify his soul and the best way to do that is to help others without selfish intentions. He says that he wants to help them. For the most part, I don't see anything that would indicate that he is lying. Like Bethany, I feel it is my duty as a good Christian Amish boy to show him the kind of compassion that we've shown you. Let's forget all of this and just get down to what we've come here for. Grab a hammer and let's put these houses back to the condition that they were in before all this happened."

I stayed close to Frankie and he was doing his best not to make eye contact with Jonathan or even get close enough for them to speak in private. I thought that he might be just one of those ones that didn't believe that Jonathan could change his ways. I then began to think that there was something more going on here than I could see with the naked eye.

"Bethany, I don't know how to tell you this, but you really shouldn't trust Jonathan as far you can throw him. He's not a good man, he's not the man that he claims to be and if you think he is, then you are deluding yourself. He wants to destroy everything that you hold dear and you're allowing him free access. You're just too damn good for your own sake. You have to have careful judgment, watch him closely and I think that you'll see that my fears are very much warranted."

"Frankie, I feel this hatred coming off of you in waves. I don't know where this animosity comes from for Jonathan, but it's not healthy. I know that you have your reservations. Myself and Jacob and even the Deacon have deemed him worthy of a chance to give back to those that he has wronged in some way. You of

43

all people know how that feels. We gave you that same courtesy after you betrayed us to El Diablo and his men. You must know that not a lot of people would do that."

"I don't care about any of that, Bethany. All I am telling you is that he can't be trusted. What you do with that information is up to you. I'm just going on record to say that I warned you." He went back to working as hard as he ever did, but he did put an inkling of a thought in my head. Were we really taking too much of a chance? Could we trust a mann that was in league with El Diablo? This was all so strange and everything that we've done up to this point had been only enough to garner the good graces of those that called this place their home.

Shtamm comes in all shapes and sizes and now Frankie's friends had a place that they could call home. They didn't have to worry about trying to find something to eat. There would be enough for everybody. I think I could say with some degree of certainty that Frankie's mistrust of Jonathan was more personal in nature. I wanted to question him further, but it didn't look like he was willing to talk. He shut down entirely, hemming and hawing, the entire time that he was working his hands raw to the bone.

Chapter 9

"I don't get it, Jacob. Frankie might be a little mistrustful of people, but Jonathan has taken that to a different level. He looks at him like he wants to kill him. He has been holding that hammer and looking at him hard. I can only imagine what's going through his head. I've tried to reach out to him, but he is reluctant to listen to me. He has warned me repeatedly that Jonathan is not somebody to be trusted. It's not like we didn't know that. We've taken precautions to make sure that he doesn't cause anybody undue harm." Frankie was somebody that had a chip on his shoulder. I could see the desire to hurt Jonathan in his eyes. The way that he handled that hammer, made me believe that he was going to go over to Jonathan and pound it into him with everything he had.

"Perhaps, I should have a talk with him mann to mann. Maybe he just needs a father figure to show him the way. If he really does have something to tell us about Jonathan, then we should do everything we can to make him feel like he can trust us with any kind of information." I should've realized that Jacob was having the same thoughts, as I was. We wanted to fix what was wrong, but I wasn't sure that was even possible.

I wasn't too far away and I even stayed close enough that I was able to overhear everything that Jacob was saying to Frankie.

"Young man, you have to learn that people can change. It's not like it's a foregone conclusion that they will stay the bad man that they are. It could be that he really does want to turn over a new leaf. We need to give him that chance. If we don't, then it doesn't make us any better than he is. Even if he is trying to trick us, then we will deal with that accordingly. As it is, he is one of our best with a hammer. I feel like he's trying to put his best foot forward for the good of everybody. Unless you have something specific that you want to tell me about Jonathan, then we have no choice, but to allow him to walk freely amongst us." I could see that Frankie wanted to say something and even opened his mouth for a moment. That soon changed and then he shut down, just as violently as he had done with me.

"I don't have anything to say and what I said to Bethany is more than enough. Just believe me when I tell you that things are not as they seen. You think that you have it all figured out and that all the pieces of the puzzle are right there for you to see. There are still some pieces that remain broken. You can't put that puzzle piece together without those broken pieces. Like I said don't come crying to me when you find out the truth." I felt his burning rage coming from his eyes. I needed to find out where all this was coming from.

"Frankie, we can't help you, unless you tell us what is on your mind." I saw him reach out to Frankie and then I saw Frankie cringe like there was a live electric wire about to touch him. "I'm not going to hurt you. Wait, did somebody hurt you? If there was, then I would like to hear it from your words." I was all ears. If anybody put a hand on him or any of the other kinner, I would be beside myself.

I moved in a little closer and I was able to hear every vivid word in detail. It made me boil with a rage that I had not felt in my life. I had to find Jonathan and show him just how I felt in a very deadly way. He couldn't hide and no matter where he went, I would find him.

I went to where I last saw him and he wasn't there. I found the Deacon and grabbed him by his collar. "I want to know where Jonathan is; you better speak up or else."

"Bethany, I've never seen you like this and maybe you should take a moment to breathe." I had no time to breathe and the only thing that I was doing was fuming. The only thing that was going to satiate that fire was having my hands around Jonathan's throat. "Nothing can be settled through violence and I think that you've seen that for yourself. You've been in league with Mitchell and his men." He didn't know what he was talking about. If he had any idea of what I heard, he would probably join me in my quest to hurt Jonathan in the worst way possible.

"Never mind, I'll find him on my own." I turned and stomped away, not even thinking about what I was going to do when I saw him. I just knew that he was going to rue the day that he had stepped into this camp with malice in his heart.

Chapter 10

The only thing I did think about was getting my hands on Jonathan and even Henry standing in front of me was no match for a woman like me. I kicked him in his ankle and he began the hop around in the kind of pain that left me to my own devices.

"Jonathan." He turned around at the sound of his name. I attacked him like a linebacker on a football team. I'd only learned about that game through some members of my flock. It was fascinating that they would be interested in something so barbaric, but it seemed to be the natural pastime of the United States.

"Bethany, I was just going to come looking for…" I didn't give them a chance to say his final thoughts, as I drove my shoulder into his midsection. The force in which I did it brought him down onto the ground and I now had him by the throat.

"You should be ashamed of yourself. Frankie told us what you did and I never imagined that you would do something like that. I've heard that it was being done, but to actually have somebody present and accountable for it is quite another thing altogether. You are a monster; these kids deserve better than somebody like you coming into their lives and turning it upside down. They deserve the kind of life that they're getting right now. You can't take that away from them, Even if you tried, I would cut you down before you had a chance to do anything. Soldiers are men and not boys that you can mold into soldiers because you were told to."

Jacob was holding my shoulders. He was trying to take my hand off his throat. I could see his eyes bulging and Jonathan was having trouble breathing. It never made me so proud in my life. I wanted to hurt him. I could almost feel myself turning into somebody like Mitchell. If he had seen me now, he would call me a hypocrite. Finally Jacob was able to release my grip by bodily force. He pulled me away and kept me from once again getting my hands on him.

"This is not the way, Bethany and we need to stop and think about this before we do anything rash." He was turned around and holding onto his throat and making these choking sounds. "You yourself know that violence is not the answer. You pulled me away from that line of thinking and I'm going to do the same thing for you. You don't have to like me and you can look at me like you hate me, but I know that it's not true."

"I didn't mean...to turn them into soldiers. It was never...my idea. I thought that I was making them peace delegates. I thought that I was...that I was doing the right thing.... I was ashamed and I still am. I need to... say something, but before I do, I think that you should be aware that there is a wolf among you."

I had no idea what he was referring to and I really was in no frame of mind to care. He was dealing with a woman that had raw emotions. A woman that was thinking about her dochtah and what she would do faced with somebody that was trying this with her. It was that fuel that was making my rage go out of control. I had to rein it on or risk losing myself like Mitchell.

"I don't care what you have to say, Jonathan. It doesn't matter to me. I think that you should leave, before I take a shovel to your head. It was a good thing that my husband was here to stop me, or this would've been lights out permanently. I want you to know that I despise you and I hope that you die miserably and alone. I hope that you die right now in front of me where I can see you writhing in agony for all eternity."

He was about to say something else, but then he looked at us with his face ashen and then blood came out of his mouth.

BOOK 10

Rachel H. Kester

This is a work of fiction. Names, characters, businesses, places, events and incidents are either the products of the author's imagination or used in a fictitious manner. Any resemblance to actual persons, living or dead, or actual events is purely coincidental.

Chapter 1

I had no idea what was going on and I thought that Jonathan was faking some sort of attack to get out of being questioned. Then I realized that the blood was real and that he would need some kind of emergency care to take care of whatever was causing him to bleed at the mouth. He was not just bleeding from just the mouth, but it was from the ears and the nose as well. Even his eyes showed droplets of that same life essence.

"I don't like the look of this, Bethany. If you were to help me, I think that we should get him to the Dr. immediately." I had no idea if we even had a Dr. The last that I knew was that the Dr. in question was now taking some leaves to be with his newfound brother. Had they been able to replace him? There was the question lingering in the air, as we made our way over to the medical tent.

"I don't know what happened. He was talking one minute and then all of sudden he was collapsing with blood coming out of everywhere. I wish that I could say that I saw something out of the ordinary, but I don't think I can." I was flustered beyond words and even

Jacob was to the point that he was panicking and sweating along his brow line.

I know that, Bethany and I was right there with you the entire time can. He was trying to say something, but then he was struck down by this mysterious illness. I hope that we are not in the mists of some kind of epidemic. We have to find out if this is serious enough and even if it is, then we need to know if it can be spread by touch or airborne methods." We had no idea what we were going to do. We could only hope that whoever was in charge in the medical tent would be able to find out what happened to him.

We went inside and we were now face to face with Nicholas. He looked completely shocked. He came towards us, not to give us a hug or a welcome of any sort, but to grab the package that we had brought him. He had a couple of nurses help him drag Jonathan over to a nearby bed. They laid him down and they stripped off his clothes using a pair of scissors. It went through the fabric and made it look like tissue paper.

He worked on him for some time and then he stood up and walked over towards us. "I'm happy to see the both of you, but I wish it was under other circumstances. What exactly happened, don't leave out any detail." We told him everything we knew and it wasn't much. "I don't know if we have anything to worry about, but first I have to determine if this is some kind of airborne pathogen that has been introduced into the atmosphere. I'm going to send out a couple of people to take some readings of the air quality and to find out if anybody else is showing any kind of symptoms."

I stepped forward "What exactly are we looking at, Nicholas?"

"If this is patient zero, then we are in luck, but if not, then there is Typhoid Mary out there somewhere spreading this amongst the people." I didn't like the sound of that and Jonathan had now turned as *weiss* as a sheet. There wasn't that much that we could do, but stand around and wait for some kind of answers to come from Nicholas. It looked like he was under a lot of pressure. I'm sure that he was going to get a lot more from the deacon.

We stayed there with him and out of the way, hoping that we could be of some kind of assistance, but finding that we were basically in the way.

"If there's anything that we can do, Nicholas, then all you have to do is ask and we will do it. He was about to say something about who was responsible for making kids turn into soldiers. We know that he was the one that ultimately did that, but somebody gave him his marching orders and we wanna know who it was." I was showing no compassion for the *mann* and I was acting like the only thing that mattered was what he could tell us. This was not the Amish way. I had turned against my beliefs, just because Mitchell had given me a reason to think that there was no hope.

"I'll be sure to call on you. Right now, all you can do is stay vigil and hopefully he will open his eyes soon and be able to tell us what has happened." Nicholas was the best of the best and I'd seen him in the field of battle. He was calm under pressure. If anybody could find out what was going on with Jonathan, it would be him. There's no denying that we had the right man for the job. I didn't even know that he was here to begin with.

"I'm happy to see you, Nicholas. I don't think that I want anybody else at this time. I just wish that you would have told us that you were coming. That you were going to join our band of merry men. I'm glad to see that you are out from underneath the shadow of Mitchell. Being with him was like putting a noose around your neck and waiting for somebody to come around to kick the chair from underneath you."

"Bethany, that is a very disturbing image, but I guess it makes sense if you think about it. Each time that I was with Mitchell, I was practically begging for a bullet to the back of the head. It wouldn't matter if I was there on a medical mission to help those that needed it most.

They would see me, as conspiring with the enemy and they would have dealt with me accordingly. I just hope that I can help this man, but so far everything that I've done has been in vain. There's something drastically wrong with him and now I believe that there's nothing to worry about concerning an epidemic."

"Are you sure, because he really did look like he was struck down by some kind of disease?"

"On further examination, Bethany, I believe that it is a poison, but which one is yet to be determined." Nicholas had done some amazing work, but there was still a whole lot more to do. If we were going to get this *mann* away from death's door, then we were all going to have to work together.

Chapter 2

I suppose people would be in their right to tell us to mind our own business, but there really was nothing more than we could do for Jonathan. He was under the care of Nicholas and that was the best place for him. Nicholas had told us that he would tell us if anything changed. We had to take him at his word and if anybody was trustworthy, it would be him. He had never shown me a reason to worry about his loyalty. If he said that he would tell us if anything changes, then I would believe that to the bottom of my heart.

"I don't know what you intend to find, Bethany, but I'm right by your side the entire time. We've just been told that it's not airborne, so at least we have not to report back to the Deacon. He'll be happy to know that this isn't some sort of epidemic that is going to run rampant through this camp. We should tell them that immediately." I thought that that was a pretty good idea. Jacob was always somebody that had a level head. It was only recently that I saw him lose it, but I guess I couldn't blame him in retrospect.

El Diablo's second in command had about just as much of the sadistic streak as he did. He didn't mind doing the dirty *schaffe* for somebody else; as long as the money was good and that he could profit and line his pockets with gold. Fighting was not the Amish way. We had been pulled into something that was beyond our control. We needed to take a stand and in doing so, we had made an enemy. The enemy was now vanquished, but that vacuum was now filled by somebody that had taken exception to us interfering in their business.

We were still rebuilding from the ashes of the fire that was left behind in the wake of El Diablo demise. We thought that we were done with this foolishness. Apparently somebody didn't want to let it go. We had no idea who that might be. Mitchell had been silent on the subject. Apparently, he had been drinking himself into a stupor and we were just waiting for him to hit rock bottom and finally ask for help.

We found everybody at the scene still standing there with their phones. I looked at Jacob and he looked at me and we had no idea what was going on. I leaned over the shoulder of one *mann* and I saw that he had videotaped the entire thing from beginning to end. The confrontation that I had with him, the choking of his throat with my hands wrapped around him and then him sputtering blood and falling face down on the ground. I'd never seen such technological marvels. I couldn't believe that anybody would be in a position to capture this for posterity.

I looked around at where the blood had soaked into the ground. There were no visible signs that there was a vial or anything broken that would determine that something had happened to him right underneath our noses.

I even looked a little further off, maybe in hopes of finding a needle or some kind of dart, but there was nothing. It had to be that it happened someplace else. That this was the catalyst to him walking around with it flowing in his veins all day. He probably didn't even know what was happening. When he succumbed, he didn't show any signs that he was visibly distressed. He didn't look in discomfort from the poison that was hitting him like a ton of bricks.

"Ladies and gentlemen, we want to inform you that Nicholas has determined that this is not anything to worry about. You are perfectly safe; this was poison and not some kind of disease that is going to take your loved ones. Go home, pray to your *Gott* and make sure that you have faith in his words and the wisdom to learn from your mistakes. Jacob and I will keep you up to date, but as it stands, it appears that somebody wanted to get him out of the way." They weren't sure if they should believe me. They turn to Jacob and saw that he was nodding his head. In a combination of my word and his, they finally made this metaphorical sigh of relief before dispersing.

"You guys really do know how to wake up the masses. I've never seen two people that stick their noses into other people's business, as much as you two do. I know that you're only doing it because you want to help. Sometimes you have to let sleeping dogs lie." The deacon was very upset and he was taking out his wrath on the both of us. I couldn't blame him, because he was right and we really didn't know when to stop.

If El Diablo was still around, we would still be out there giving him heck. He would never know when we were going to strike next, but thankfully we didn't have that particular problem to deal with any more.

"We're sorry you feel that way, Deacon. My husband and I were just trying to make this world a better place. You can say that you would have turned the other cheek. You don't know that, until you're into a position where you have to learn about yourself. Jacob and I have done that and I don't think that you really want to know some of the details." He turned around and waved his hands in the air into surrendering motion. He was shaking his head in disbelief and walking away probably thinking that he had done us wrong in some way.

"Don't get me wrong, Bethany, but I really do like the Deacon, but sometimes he can really churn my butter." Such language coming from a *mann* of catholic upbringing. "Pardon my French, but frankly he doesn't know a good thing when it's staring him in the face." I'd gone around and confiscated all the phones and some were unwilling, but they were quickly convinced that it was in their best interest.

We sat on the ground and Jacob and I watched the footage of each and every one of them. We wanted to see something out of the ordinary, but there was absolutely nothing to see. It was exactly what we had seen for ourselves with our own eyes. He had been attacked by me, I had choked him and then out of the blue, he began to sputter blood. At first, I thought that I was responsible, but after seeing him bleeding from other places, I knew that I couldn't be.

"I don't know if I understand why anybody would want to take videos of something that they are seeing with their own eyes."

"Bethany, we will never understand how western civilization thinks. They always seem to want to go that extra mile in technology and sometimes there's something to say for the simpler kind of life. Living with you and your *dochtah* has been a godsend. My finding you as my wife has been nothing, but a miracle." It was nice to hear him say that once in awhile.

Chapter 3

"I don't know about you, Jacob, but I'm tired of looking at these videos. We've been looking at them for over 3 hours and I think my eyes have crossed to a point that I'm feeling at a loss for words. I need to take a break and if you want to continue, then by all means do so." I felt like I was going around in circles. There was no end in sight. I've heard nothing from Nicholas in all this time and I was beginning to worry that he was at a loss and couldn't find what was making Jonathan sick.

"Bethany, you go and get something to eat and if I need anything, I'll come and join you. Don't worry about me; I'm just trying to get a handle on this thing. There has to be something in here that we're missing. It's probably something, so small that we wouldn't even recognize it, unless we were seriously looking for it." I didn't understand what he was saying. Jacob and I had been mulling over this for hours. We needed to take a break and if need be, we could come back and take a look at it again.

"I'll bring you back some *kaffe*, because I know how you like it strong and black. I've made sure to give them the recipe of your *daett*. You can imagine that they were not very happy with how strong it is. It does increase productivity by at least 50%. I've seen the results for myself and most people feel, so wired that they can't sit still for hours. We need that jolt right about now. I just pray to *Gott* that there's enough there at this time of night." I wasn't even sure if I could find any kind of sustenance. The cook would most likely be fast asleep in his bed by now.

I walked casually across the camp and I looked at the tent flaps and I could imagine each and every one of these people thinking the worst. In the back of their mind, they would know that there was nothing to worry about. There would always be that nagging doubt sinking in and telling them something different. Some of them were probably even contemplating taking off in the morning. I would have to be there to intervene and show them that they didn't have to go to that extreme.

I went into the mess hall and I saw that there was only one person there and it turned out to be Nicholas. He was chewing on a sandwich and it looked like it was tough. He continually had to move his jaws over and over again. "Bethany, it's nice to see you; maybe you can tell me why this roast beef taste like shoe leather." He had a cup of the *kaffe* that I had mentioned to Jacob, right in front of him. It was steaming hot. I looked to the pot to see that there was probably just enough there for two more cups.

I poured myself one. I was going to go and get Jacob one after I had finished talking to Nicholas. "The roast beef taste like shoe leather, because it has probably been there for the last five days. Let's just say that the cook likes to use everything. If there are leftovers, then you can be assured that the next day you're going to be eating the very same thing. He doesn't like to waste any thing. Apparently he is one of these Haitians that believe that wasting something was like a cardinal sin." I sat down and he was still eating, but in front of him were these files with all sorts of numbers.

"I don't like somebody reading over my shoulder, Bethany, but for you I will make an exception. I don't think that you'll understand any of this, but for the most part, I've done preliminary tests. I've done everything I can, but I know that there's more that I can do. Tomorrow, I'm going to start using the Internet. I've already talked to the Deacon. He has given me permission to tap into the local wifi signal. I have all of these damn books on poisons and I know that the answer is in there somewhere. His symptoms could be one of a number of poisons out there. If I can narrow it down, I should be able to find some kind of cure."

He looked frazzled and his hair was matted with sweat. He didn't look like he had slept for days. "Why not just give him the cure for each and every one of them. Eventually one of them will be the right one." I saw him cock an eyebrow and I had a feeling like I said something wrong.

"Don't get me wrong, I understand that you don't know a whole lot about medicine. You wouldn't know that from the way that you conducted yourself on the battlefield. Your compassion leads to helping others. I still say that you could make a remarkable Dr. or even a nurse. Anyway, if I were to give him any of those cures without knowing what the poison was, it's very possible that I would kill him. Some of these cures are very potent. I've been racking my brain. I'm starting to see pretty little lines in front of my eyes. I'm going to have to take a break from this and come back at it fresh in the morning."

I was just thinking the same thing about Jacob and I perusing over those videos. "I know that you are frustrated, but try to keep a stiff upper lip. I don't know where that came from. I think it was from that English exchange student that was here on loan from across the pond. I mean, I just want you to continue to fight and never give up. You are a professional and you are a Dr. and there is respect from me in what you do." He still didn't look convinced. He gave me a small smile, before walking out with those files in hand and a cup of *kaffe* skill clutched in other one.

I went over to the pot and poured the remaining bit into a cup. I knew that this would be the strongest of them all. It was the last of the pot. The bit at the bottom would be the most intense. I took a sip and I scrunched up my face, knowing full well that Jacob would love to have this kind of lead running through his veins.

I walked away and I went back outside to feel a slight sprinkle of rain. It was good to feel. We needed something to wash away this ugliness. We also needed something for the crops. It had been a hard time getting enough moisture into this clay like surface to make anything grow. I did notice that the kids were lending a hand and apparently they were quite good at gardening. It would stand to reason, because they were being taught to be self sufficient and one of those things to self sufficient was growing your own food.

Chapter 4

I awoke at 4:00 AM to see that Jacob was still up. I went to him and casually put my hand on his shoulder. "I think that it's time that you give this up. There's nothing there to see. Even if there is, you're not going to see it, until you get some rest. Come back to bed, I miss you by my side." I felt alone and I didn't like that feeling. I reminded me of when I lost my husband and I had to sleep with the knowledge that he would never be there by my side again. This was not a feeling that I wanted to repeat and yet Jacob was starting to make me feel that way.

"I don't want to do anything to cause you to feel that way, Bethany. I know that what you say is true, but it doesn't make it easier to walk away." Jacob finally picked himself up. He came over and laid his head on the pillow. The cold earth was our mattress and we had gotten used to it. It took a bit of doing, but our bodies became accustomed to the hard packed feeling up against our back. We did have sleeping bags and we did use them on occasion, but most times we just lay there with the two pillows and the feel of our fingers touching each other.

I would put my head on his chest and listen to his heartbeat. It would lull me into a sense of security. This was no different and I felt infinitely better than I did when he wasn't in bed with me. I actually found myself falling asleep and waking to see that he had done the same. We needed this more than we could know. By the time we finally roused from our slumber it was 5 hours later. It was 9:00 AM and nobody had come to get us for our shift with the hammers. Apparently, they had been told not to bother us and that we were up all night trying to find some answers.

"I hope that you're feeling better, Jacob. I just had an idea that might amount to finding out what did this to Jonathan." It was almost like a light bulb going off over my head and I had to admit that a little rest goes a long way.

"Don't leave me in suspense. I've been trying to think of something that will lead to answers, but I don't know anything that will." He was still frustrated, but at least he was well rested and ready to step back into the light. Darkness was not our friend and at night, I feel my own demons coming back to haunt me. I try to go to bed before 8:00 PM, because I didn't want that sense of melancholy to wash over me like a warm blanket.

"I think that we should gather up some volunteers and go search his belongings. He was only here a short time. He was given his own tent, because nobody else would want to be with him. I know that it's in bad taste to disturb his privacy, but I don't think we have any other choice." I watched Jacob nod his head and then he followed me out and we gathered a few likeminded individuals that were willing to get their hands dirty.

One of them was Nicholas. He wanted to be there in case something caught his eye. We went inside and there was very little there to search. There was one lone green bag and looking through it, we found a few rations, some clothes, but nothing really to indicate that he was the monster that he had been. Whatever he was now, he had shied away from his other destructive side and decided to go on the road leading to salvation.

I found a letter, but it didn't look all that important, until I opened it and began to read it aloud.

"I don't know how I got stuck here in the middle of Haiti doing the devils work, but I don't feel good about it. These kids deserve better, but if I try to talk back or show any kind of sign that I am thinking for myself, then El Diablo is going to take action. He knows where my family lives. There were several occasions that he told me that he would use them against me. He never said that he would kill them, but I could see the look in his eyes and I know that that is his intention. All I can hope is that I can walk away from this one day without blood on my hands. I know that that is a horrible thing to say, but I don't want to live with those faces in my dreams." I perused some more, but for the most part, he was a struggling with his own convictions and basically was in between a rock and a hard place.

"Bethany, I would say that this man has been fighting his true self for a very long time. There's no denying that he has done some wrongs, but he has been doing everything he can to make it right. You should see that in this letter and if you read the last passage, you'll know that he was ready to make a clean start." I would say that Nicholas was the one that has reading more into his words. I was finding out that Jonathan has moral convictions.

I took the letter from Nicholas's hands and I went down to the very last passage to read from what would be considered the last words of a possible dead man.

"My son has reminded me that life is about the choices that we make and I'm about to walk away. I'm glad to see that El Diablo has been dealt with, but that leaves me in a quandary. I could stay here and try to mend some fences, or I can go home and find you…my son and give you a big hug and kiss. I don't know which way I'm going to go, but I do have a lot to make up for. I don't think it would be right for me to just run in the opposite direction." The letter was very telling and I felt sort of bad for putting my hands around his throat.

I should've realized that there was more to his story than met the eye. I was now getting a bird's eye view of what made the *mann*.

Chapter 5

"Jacob, I feel kind of bad about attacking Jonathan like that. I didn't know what he was going through. Apparently he was struggling with some internal problems. He didn't want to be the bad guy, but he was put into a position where he didn't know what to do. He was protecting his family and I'm not sure if I would've done anything different. If anybody had told me that they were going to kill my *dochtah* Rebekah, I probably would've done anything to prevent it."

"Bethany, I'm glad that you didn't have to go through what that *mann* did. He's obviously beating himself up and this was his punishment to make some kind of penance for what he has done. I have to give him credit for having the courage to come forward and tell us that he was responsible for some of the heinous acts El Diablo was given credit for. He could've easily just kept his mouth shut, but that was not the kind of *mann* that he was. I mean the *mann* that he is. To talk about him in the past tense means that we have given up. I will never do that and he deserves better than that. He deserves our best and I know that both of us will never stop fighting for him as long as he lives." We were standing hand in hand over by the brook and I just finished giving my sermon for the day. It was about how somebody could lose his way and then through faith and conviction that they could find their way back to the path that they were supposed to be on.

I was certain that that was what happened to Jonathan. I could not in good conscience let him slip through this mortal coil without at least giving it my all and then some.

We walked back and we stopped at the tents to see that Nicholas was a lot more jovial than he was the last time I saw him. He looked despondent before, like he had lost his best friend and didn't know what to do about it.

"You two are the ones that I want to see. If anybody can help me with this, then I trust you more than anybody. I figured out that it is a poison, but I think I found something that has determined the way that he was given it." We went closer and he used a very large magnifying glass overhead to show us this red blotch with a hole in the middle of it. It was on his neck at the back of his spine. "I believe that he was punctured with some sort of needle and I would say from the discoloration that it would have to have happened in the last 24 hours." For that time, he was here inside this camp, so that meant that somebody was amongst us wearing sheep's clothing, as a wolf.

"I don't even want to believe that somebody is here and doing such things. It goes against everything we believe in and I've gotten to know these people intimately. I don't think that I could even imagine that one of them would be responsible for something like this. I guess we really don't know what goes on in somebody's mind." I was trying to go through a list of the people in my head, but so far nothing jumped out at me.

"That's only part of what I found and the other part is more uplifting. I believe that I've narrowed down the search of the poisons to 12. I would say that we should find out which one it is, but I think it would be easier if we were to find out which one it isn't.

"I think I know what you are going to ask and we'd be happy to take six each and go through the symptoms and see which one matches up the best." He handed me a leaflet of paper and then he tore it in half and passed the other part to Jacob.

"I would do it myself, but I'm still working with some professionals on the Internet. That will keep my undivided attention on that alone. You have to know that they were instrumental in helping me narrow it down to those 12. We are discussing how I'm going to precede in treating my patient. There are different opinions."

Jacob and I went through what we had. We started to check off one at a time. It was painstaking *schaffe*, but it was worth it. It might show us the way to help a fallen soldier in the field of battle. To me, he was a hero and for him to walk away with the risk of his son feeling the wrath of whoever was going to pick up the mantle of power was admirable. He deserved my respect. I was beginning to see that even Mitchell was lost and needed somebody to come by with a helping hand to show him the way. I had shunned him, turned him towards the bottle and that was a cross that I was going to have to bear.

I looked over to see the Nicholas had a screen with at least six individuals talking all at the same time. I couldn't be easy to follow one conversation or the other. For him to do that was showing to me and everybody else that he was willing to do practically anything for somebody that had been stricken down.

Chapter 6

"YIPPEEEEE!" We both turned to see that Nicholas throwing his papers in the air. He looked like he had come with some sort of breakthrough "I can't believe that this might work. If it does, then I owe you big time. Trust me, when I'm back in the States, we'll get together and I'll show you who is going to be able to drink who underneath the table. OK, I have to get back to my patient. I appreciate all the kind words and your help in this regard." We couldn't hear the other side of the conversation, but he seemed relatively happy by the conclusion of the conference call.

I looked over at Jacob and he had whittled his down to four and I had mine down to three. It meant that we had knocked off five of the 12. It wasn't close enough yet, but we still had some more *schaffe* to do.

"I would say from the look on your face that things are looking up." I was using positive thinking.

"I just got off with a few colleagues and one in England has given me an idea that might just give him a fighting chance. He's going to need a blood transfusion. I'm going to have to go through the records to find out who matches him. I know that he is a rare blood type and that in itself is going to be a major obstacle to overcome. I'm just glad that it's possible that a blood transfusion will slow down the progress of the poison and hopefully that will be long enough for us to find a cure."

"Nicholas, we have some interesting news as well. We have narrowed it down to seven and the other five has one particular symptom that's not part of what Jonathan is going through. It's only reason why we have knocked it off the list. As it is, it's still a giant leap for the one that we're looking for, but at least we're making progress. With this transfusion, maybe we might be able to do what you said and find a cure and give it to him before it's too late." I didn't think that he was listening to me, because he was now perusing the files of each and every one that was inside this camp. Everybody was required to go through a certain battery of blood tests, including the new arrivals that had just got here recently.

"I'll be damned." I didn't like his choice of phrase, but I guess he was not as religious as either myself or Jacob. "There is one person in this camp that has what he needs and it's one of the kids that we brought back from the orphanage. His name is Thomas and I believe that we need to have a frank discussion with him immediately, if not sooner." It was in the middle of the day and finding him wouldn't be all that hard to do.

We went in search of Thomas. We really didn't know what he looked like. I figured that my new charge would know him implicitly. Frankie was with them through everything that they had to go through, including the death of the one that protected them.

I found him hard at *schaffe*, as usual at one of the sites. He looked at me and I think he knew that something was up.

"Before you say anything, Bethany, I want you to know that I am appreciative of everything that you've done for me. I really don't want to get involved with anybody else's business. I know that you and Jacob have a hard time leaving things alone, but I'm not like that. I would rather be left alone and I would appreciate that you abide by my wishes."

"Normally, I would be happy to do that, but a *mann's* life is on the line. I need to get in touch with Thomas." At the sound of his name, Frankie looked at me and then he began to shake his head like he couldn't believe that I was actually asking him to intervene on my behalf "The *mann* is Jonathan and he's the one that you said that couldn't be trusted. I want you to read this letter and tell me that he doesn't have some redeeming qualities." I handed him the letter. He read it from the top to bottom. He handed it back over to me.

"I can't promise anything, but I do know where he might be at this time of day. Let me do the talking, because he only sees adults as a nuisance. I was under the same sentiment, but you changed me. I'm not sure if I like that or hate that. I believe I said that before, but you do seem to have a way of getting under my skin." I followed him and we found Thomas exactly where Frankie believed him to be. He was sitting by the same tree that I had been earlier. I guess he found it soothing to hear the bubbling brook and to stand there with the sun beating down on his face.

I could see that there was a hardened feeling coming from the kid and I really didn't think that he would be receptive to my advances. He was one of those that took the word of somebody that he trusted over the adults with more experience.

"Like I said, Bethany, I'll talk to him, but I'm not promising anything. He has always had a bit of an aversion to helping others. I guess that's the reason why we are friends. We're not exactly friends, but we do respect each other and that is more than I get from anybody else. Present company excluded. Trust me, if I can convince him, I will, but it's not gonna be easy. He obviously going to feel trapped and I don't want him to think that he's obligated to do anything. Just promise me that if he says no that you won't force him by bodily harm." I wasn't sure if I could make that allowance, but if I didn't, then I wouldn't be any better than El Diablo.

Chapter 7

"I just want you to do your best and think of Jonathan that fights for his life at this time. He could have easily succumbed by now, but he is a fighter. He needs us to do the same for him." I didn't want to play the guilt card, but he needed to know just how important it was that we got through to the kid.

"I don't like this, Bethany, but I told you that I would try and that is all that I'm going to do. I'll make my plea and you can even listen. Go over by that tree in the shadows. You'll be able to hear everything that I'm saying. It should give you an understanding about who Thomas is. He's really a good kid. He might've had to grow up quickly, but at least he didn't turn into a monster. He could have easily gone down another path. It would've been easier than struggling for everything in his life. I could've done the same thing; I did make a momentary mistake by announcing your presence to El Diablo and his men."

"I told you that I forgave you for that and I would never hold that against you." He nodded his head and then walked over to the kid and knelt down at his side. I moved to the very spot that he told me to and I could hear them crystal clear. The wind was carrying their voices and I think that Frankie knew that somehow.

"Thomas, I need to ask you something, but first you have to know how dire the circumstances are. Jonathan, the one that came here with his hand out and his hat in his hand has fallen victim to a poison that is now ravaging his body and killing him with each second that passes. "

"Frankie, I don't know why that concerns me. I believe that you might be getting a little soft. You obviously have a connection to Bethany and Jacob and maybe you should stop thinking that you're safe, when you're not. That man does not deserve our help and I don't care if he begs for it. He'll die and I'll smile and dance on his grave." That was pretty harsh words and this was coming from a kid and not a full grown adult.

"I understand your mistrust of these people and I was right there with you, until Bethany told me that she forgave me for turning them in to El Diablo. I never thought that anybody would be that forgiving. I guess I respect them for that. If you don't help, then this man will die and the truth will die with him. This whole thing can be prevented by just a few drops of your blood." I think he was underplaying it slightly, because it was going to be slightly more than just a few droplets of his blood.

"I don't know what you want me to say and I think that I'm going to need some time to think about this. Come with me. Also, you can tell your friend Bethany that I know that she's there; she can come along if she wants to." There was definite venom in between each of his words. If I didn't know any better, I would say that he was happy to see that Jonathan was close to the end of his life cycle.

I met up with Jacob and myself and Frankie went with him and followed Thomas down to the brook. He began to skip stones, staring at the glassy service and most likely thinking about what he was going to do.

"I see that you've found him, but has he agreed to help?" I think the answer was obvious, but I turned and shrugged my shoulders to indicate that it was still up in the air. "I just talked to Nicholas and he says that he's slipping further and he's going to need that blood transfusions sooner rather than later." I understood the severity and the urgency of what we had to accomplish. It wasn't like I could just go down there and slap the taste out of the kid's mouth. No matter how much I wanted to shake him and tell him that he had to get over whatever it was he was feeling towards Jonathan. I didn't do that. It would be wrong and I had to treat them like they were individuals.

"I told you Bethany that he was going to be a tough nut to crack. Something happened to him and he has been carrying it like a torch ever since. I saw it as plain as day on his face when he came to the orphanage with bruises on his face. It looked like he had been in a fight. He has never spoken of it and we didn't try to push the issue. We believed that he would come to us and tell us in his own time. Then you came around after our protector died and his voice was never heard from again." Frankie was trying to give us insight into the kids mindset.

"I hope you know, Bethany that if he doesn't decide to help then I might have to do something drastic. I'm a lot stronger than him and I could pin him down and take the blood by force, but I really don't wanna do that. He'll most likely hate me for it and then run off in the middle of the night to get himself killed." Jacob was not going to allow his indecision to stand in the way and I could only hope that the kid would see his responsibility for human life.

"I don't know what he's going to do, but I hope for all of our sake that he makes the right decision." I held the Bible in my hand and looked towards it and then to the heavens above to ask for some kind of guidance. I prayed to *Gott* that he would give this kid the answer that he was seeking. Suddenly, his back went straight and he dropped the rock that was in his hand. He was now facing us like a man.

"I've made my decision and I think that I found a perfect compromise.

Chapter 8

"I'll give you 1 hour to get what you want from me. After that you don't get any more. I don't care if you come begging on your hands and knees. This is my terms and I'm not going to back down." I guess we could take solace in the fact that he was willing to help at all. Something had obviously happened to give this kid and skewed opinion of the *mann* that was fighting for his life. "If you can live with that, then I'll be more than happy to help you." It didn't sound like he was happy. It sounded like he was just doing it because he felt like he was obligated to do so.

"I'm glad to see that you are willing, but maybe if you get that chip off your shoulder you would feel better. Why don't you tell us why you're, so angry at Jonathan? I know that he's done some bad things, but I had no idea that you knew anything of it." He looked to me sternly. I thought for sure that he was going to scream. He turned his back and began to tell us a story that had us at the edge of our seat.

"I really don't know where to begin, so I suppose I just start at the beginning. My brother and I were taken from our homes by force by El Diablo's men and we were given a choice. We could either die with our parents, or we could learn to be soldiers. We had to watch, as they literally cut off the heads of our mother and father. We were living on a dam farm in the middle of nowhere, where they shouldn't have been able to find us, but they did. My older brother tried to keep me from going insane and for the most part he was able to accomplish that task.

"It sounds to me like you've been through hell and I'm amazed that you are able to stand. You should be in the fetal position rocking back and forth and muttering things underneath your breath. It can't even imagine what that must have felt like to see your parents die like that. I would never wish that on my worst enemy."

"Anyway, we were taken to their camps and we were not the only ones. There were several young up and coming soldiers that had been forced to do the same thing that we were. One of those soldiers had decided to make a break for it. When they were brought back, they were shown just what their actions would cause to others. El Diablo with that death mask on stood behind my brother and shot him in the head. He didn't do it because my brother betrayed him; he did it because he was making an example of him, so that no other soldier would try to run."

"I don't know what to say. For you to carry that with you all the time must be a little unnerving." I wanted to take the kid in my arms and shelter him from the world. I couldn't do that, because he was not a little boy. In his eyes, you could see that the man had been born out of necessity. "You're very strong and I would've been proud to have you as my son. You don't give up, you never surrender and you always keep moving forward, because there is no other choice."

"Bethany, I appreciate your kind words, but they are unnecessary. In the middle of the night, I scratched my way out of the barracks. I made my way over to the fence and was accosted by a guard and got into a scuffle. We fought tooth and nail and I got the worst of it. He thought that he had me exactly where he wanted me. I was sniveling like a coward, but then I grabbed the first thing that I could find and smacked it up side his face. He died on the impact of that rock striking against his skull. I left him to stare at the sky. I went underneath the fence and ran with everything I had. I don't think that my brother would be very proud of me." He looked like he was boiling with rage, but he allowed us to take him to the medical tent.

"We have some good news, Dr...." I didn't get a chance to say much more, because the Dr. was already very busy.

"I'm afraid that it might be too late. He's gone downhill quickly and I had to induce a coma in order to keep him alive longer. I don't even know if the transfusion is going to work anymore, but I still want to give it a shot." Thomas didn't even try to fight. He showed no emotion whatsoever during the procedure. He didn't cry out when the needle was puncturing into his skin and all he would do was stare straight ahead and wait for it to be over.

This kid was the real hero and we all could take lessons from the bravery that he had shown in the face of true evil. He was lucky that he got out of it, or El Diablo would've taken great pride in taking his head along with his brothers. There was no rhyme or reason for EL Diablo's actions, only that they were reprehensible and that his death was too good for him.

Chapter 9

"I don't know if one transfusion is going to do it. I did find something that might be useful, but it's only useful if we can find it in time." Nicholas showed us that there was a rare flower out there in the wilderness that could be the cure that we were looking for. "I don't even know if it's going to work, but it's his best chance for survival. The only problem is, I've talked to the locals and they are unwilling to go out there to retrieve this particular flower. They say that it is poisonous. I've tried to convince them otherwise, but they are steadfast in their belief."

"Nicholas, Jacob and I would be happy to go. Just give us a photograph of what it looks like and maybe a brief outline or description." He told us that it had a prickly thorn and the photo showed a purple blossom that had a white interior.

"What you're looking for is the petals. They are going to be used to boil down into a tea. As long as I can get him to drink it, then it might be able to ward off the poison. This flower is said to have some amazing properties. I think that whoever did this to him suspected that the locals would not want to volunteer their services to go and retrieve it. They were banking on that, but they didn't know that there were two people that did not believe in such superstition."

I looked over at Thomas and he was pale and barely able to keep his eyes open. It was time to relieve him of the needle, but when I went to take it out, he stopped me with his hand on my wrist.

"I can't let you do that and I promised that I would give you everything I could and I'm not there yet. I also said that this would be the only time that you would be able to get any of this from me. That is something that I plan to follow through on. It's the only reason why I'm staying here longer than necessary. I'll crawl out of here on my hands and knees if I have to, but this is your one and only shot." He was a determined young kid and if he wanted to go a little further, then who was I to say that he couldn't?

"You do what you have to do, Thomas. We'll do what we have to. I just don't want you to go too far, because we don't want to lose you as well. I'm hoping that you'll know when enough is enough. You'll make that decision on your own. If you were to pass out, then the decision would be left in Nicholas's hands." He was close to passing out as it was, but he was struggling and fighting the urge to sleep with every fiber of his being.

Jacob and I walked over to the forest and started to make our way through with the use of a machete that we had borrowed from one of the locals. He began to chop his way through, leaving a path of destruction to the weeds that were in the way. I saw his eyes and knew that he wasn't going to give up, until he found that flower by any means necessary.

"Jacob, you don't have anything to prove and we'll just do our best and let *Gott* sort out the rest." He smiled, but that didn't stop him from pushing forward. He was not allowing even a snake to stand in his way. He chopped the head off and it was still hissing with its tail pointed up. The head had been separated from its body.

"I would never have killed it, but it was showing signs that it was going to attack. If something wants to live, then they will leave me alone, or otherwise I will have to make them regret it." I don't know why it was so important to him, but maybe the story that Thomas had told had lit a fire underneath him the likes that I had never seen before.

Chapter 10

I was watching my husband in action and he was slashing his way with the machete. It made me proud to know that he would always be there for me. "Jacob, you are amazing and I don't know how many times I've told you today that I love you."

He stopped momentarily, turned and embraced me. He had me wishing that we could stay here forever. "I know that, Bethany and I think I wake up every morning thanking *Gott* that I am with you. We've been through a lot and we're always been there for each other and that will never end. This is the kind of love that will stand up to the test of time." We stayed there for a moment longer, before he made this sigh of resignation and turned to start swiping at these long blades of grass in the way.

As he was doing that, I was looking around and following him at the same time. I noticed something out of the corner of my eye. I went toward it and just like that I was peering at this flower. I looked at the photograph and then to Jacob and then he sliced that flower away from the branch. We put it into a small burlap sack and then turned to see that the path that we had made was there waiting for us to make our return.

It had been a good 20 minutes and it took that long and a bit longer to get back. We had exactly what Jonathan needed and then we entered into the tent to hear the telltale sign of beeping.

"He's flat lighting… somebody bring me the paddles." it looked like our efforts were in vain. We watched in horror as Nicholas tried his best to revive Jonathan. It look like it was a lost cause and then, as a last ditch effort, Jonathan bought his fist down on top of the Jonathan's chest. Nicholas lay on top of him with his head on his chest and then his eyes came alive and he looked up to see that the beeping had now become an erratic pattern instead.

"I can't believe it. I was almost ready to give up and now he's back with us. Give me that flower and let's get that thing boiled down into a tea, as quick as possible." One of the locals had decided that their guilt was getting the best of them. They were right here to help us with the tea. He made in the traditional way. Once it was done, we took it over to Jonathan and propped his head up on pillows and placed it against his lips.

Jacob held his nose and I poured the concoction into his mouth. He began to choke, but at least it was going down. We managed to get him to drink the entire thing. It was just a matter of waiting.

We stayed at his bedside, not sleeping for 12 hours. His eyes finally blinked open. He tried to speak, but he couldn't. Questions could wait till later and right now we were just happy to have him alive and kicking.

The poison had been cleansed and Nicholas had confirmed that his blood work was showing remarkable improvement.

"I don't know what happened, but I was in the process of telling you that the person that was responsible for making me turn the kids in the soldiers was a woman. You wouldn't know it to look at her, but she was evil. She didn't care about these kids feelings and when they got out of line, she hit them with this switch that left permanent marks. I wanted to stop her, but she was a force on to herself. I don't know where El Diablo found her, but she was like his counterpart. They were perfectly suited to each other." He gave us a description and I listened to it intently. I still couldn't believe what I was hearing. The woman that he was describing had a remarkable resemblance to…Gabrielle.

BOOK 11

Rachel H. Kester

Chapter 1

It was good to see Jonathan back up on his feet. Nicholas had been doing tests on him for the last few hours. The cure was only a folk tale that was passed down from the Haitian community. He looked like he was in good spirits and even though he was walking on shaky legs, didn't mean that he wasn't going to make a recovery.

It's nice to see you up and about, Jonathan. I just want to be the first one to apologize for my behavior. I'm afraid that my emotions got the best of me. I hope that you won't hold that against me. I do have an ulterior motive for coming and seeing you like this." He looked at me and smiled and that made me feel good.

Bethany, you have nothing to apologize for. You found out about a piece of my past and I can't fault you for that. I can't even be mad at you for attacking me and trying to choke the life out of me. I would've done the same thing in your shoes. I'm sure that anybody else would have done the same thing. You probably surprised yourself by doing something like that. I'm just angry at myself that I had to put you in that position."

I'm very appreciative for your understanding, Jonathan."

Bethany, I understand that you have an ulterior motive. I know that you have some questions about the woman. They call her the angel of death and I watched her train and humiliate those that were under her command. She was ruthless, domineering and if I didn't know any better, I would say that she was just as bad as El Diablo or maybe more so." This was not good news and if Gabrielle was really responsible for this, then I needed to know. The description that he had given could be Gabrielle. Until I saw with my own eyes, I wouldn't believe it, because I couldn't believe it.

I felt a hand on my shoulder and I knew immediately that it was Jacob my beloved. He had just finished hard *schaffe* with one of the houses. His spirits were looking like they were coming back to where they were before all of his hard *schaffe* was turned to ashes.

I was just telling your wife that the angel of death is not somebody that you should be messing with. She's still out there. I may have walked away, but I don't think I did it unscathed. I think we all know that she was responsible in some way for giving me that needle. I understand that they found out who did it and when they went looking for him, he disappeared. I think you can see by now that the angel of death has her reach into just about everything, every… oh my. I caught him before he fell and Jacob was right there to lend the assistance of his manly muscles.

Jonathan, you just have to take it easy. I'm going to go talk to Nicholas and see if he can't shed some light on this. Jacob and I left him to deal with his rehab, he was wearing a pair of blue sleep pants and a pullover white shirt. He still looked a little pale, but at least he was a walking and talking. That was a far cry from where he was a few hours ago.

I went into the tent and I found Nicholas very happy. He was typing madly on the computer and he looked up and clapped his hands. You won't believe this, but that flower is now going to be used to extract a cure. It will be placed into a database for the CDC. They've never seen this kind of poison before and they were most anxious to get their hands on it to do some necessary research. I know it's morbid, but they are going to name it after me."

That's great, but we want to discuss something else." He looked up and now it was time to find out if he could help us. We were wondering if you could reach out to Mitchell and his men. We want to find out if they know anything about this angel of death. A photo would be preferable, but I'm not exactly sure if that's possible." He promised that he would look into it, but he didn't know if Mitchell was going to be in any shape to help anybody.

I told you that Mitchell has been going downhill. I'm not sure if he's going to be able to make it back from the demons that have been haunting him. I understand that this is very important to you. It must be a little disconcerting to realize that a woman that you tried to help was responsible for making kids do things that would scar them for life. I'll try and reach out to his second in command. It's the only way that we're going to get their assistance. To tell you the truth, I don't like Mitchell's second in command. He has a different style than Mitchell."

I would have to find a way to get a chance to delve into that story and I was sure that there was a story behind it. We left the tent and we found that Jonathan was being helped by a couple of the locals. Even a couple of our own community had decided to lend a hand. I would say that Jonathan's days of having the cold shoulder were over. It was possible that he could find redemption for his lost soul.

Chapter 2

While Nicholas was reaching out to Mitchell's second in command and possibly Mitchell himself, Jacob and I had *schaffe* to do. The kinner were running around having the time of their lives. Those that were responsible for them were making sure that they were well fed and had a roof over their head. I was quite impressed by how well they bounced back. Kinner usually have a way of taking things and dealing with them quickly. Some were a little too young to even remember. Hopefully in a few months the painful realization that they were living hand to mouth would be gone for good.

Bethany, I know what you're thinking. I see them and I think of all the things that they had to go through and it chills me to the very bone. I'm glad that they had you to lean on. We were able to find them suitable homes. They've lost a lot, but now they have gained a new family and that is more than they probably hoped would ever happen." Jacob took off his hat and the brau colored fabric looked faded from his sweat and the hard *schaffe* that he had been doing.

You know, you don't have to hold all of this on your shoulders yourself, Jacob. I'm here with you and all of these people are willing and able to lift the hammer to do their part. I see even Jonathan has signed up to get back to it." I could see him drinking hot *kaffe* and apparently it was laced with more of the antidote. I've heard through Nicholas that he was going to have to continue this regiment of drinking this stuff for the next two weeks. One of the Elders from the Haitian community had decided to oversee his recovery. She was elderly, but she was strong and firm and very strict in what she demanded.

I'm drinking it; you don't have to browbeat me into it." She was pointing her finger into his chest. For a girl that didn't measure more than 5'2, she was a firecracker and a force to be reckoned with.

We made our way back over to Nicholas and he was standing there in front of the medical tent. He was actually smoking. He looked at me and realized that he had been caught in the act. He looked sheepishly at his shoes and then dropped the butt at his feet. He stomped it out. He then looked back up feeling slightly guilty about his habit.

I tried to quit five years ago. I was doing so well, until I came here with Mitchell and everything changed. I needed to relieve myself of some of the frustration of the day. It calms me and I know that they're cancer sticks waiting to kill me. My body craves it and there's no way that I can deny myself that moment of peace in the middle of all this chaos." I was going to have to help him with that addiction.

If you want help, then all you have to do is ask. I won't try to force anything on you and I've learned in the past that people have to reach out first. Then and only then can I help them find their way to get that monkey off their back" My *daett* had that problem and so did a couple of his friends. They had gotten their hand on tobacco. I was instrumental in giving them their lives back. I couldn't stop one and before long, he was succumbing to the effects. Thankfully, it wasn't my *daett*. I was quite happy that I had given him a new lease on life.

I was grateful for my *maemm* in law that she was taking care of my *dochtah* Rebekah and making sure that she was fed and clothed and feeling loved. I was doing my best to send good vibes their way. Whenever I had them on the phone, I made sure to let Rebekah knew that I would always be in her life. The last time, I could feel this wave of anger coming across the airwaves. She was obviously missing me and at one point I was going to have to take her feelings into account.

I've tried to reach Mitchell, but people have told me that it's not worth my time. He's too far gone and he has literally walked away from his mission and his duty. He spends his days in a bar drinking and making a complete disgrace of himself. However, his second command was very anxious to hear about what we found out about the angel of death. He didn't know much, but he did hear rumors of a person that fit that description to a tee. It was being discussed in hushed terms and he had to pry some loose lips to get the information." This angel of death was now the one that was taken the place of El Diablo. With that vacuum filled, it wouldn't be long before she started to branch out her territory all over again.

I think for the well being of everybody, we should go to Mitchell ourselves and see if we can't do anything to give him back his life. After everything that happened with Jonathan, I now realize that things are not as black and white as they appear. I want to give him the benefit of doubt. It's time that I finally let sleeping dogs lie."

Bethany, we both know that Nicholas can't go with us. He has *schaffe* here to do. Besides, I don't think he wants to revisit his past again." I could see that Nicholas was shaking his head; this was his way of telling us that he had no interest in coming with us. I'll tell the Deacon that we're taking a short sabbatical. I'll pass off my duties to Maxwell. He's shown some remarkable fortitude when it comes to carpentry. He is a bit of an idiot savant." Jacob didn't have to come with me, but I knew that I would never be able to go alone. He would follow me and there would be nothing that I could do to prevent him from walking back in to the danger again. We couldn't risk anybody else with us. This is my cross to bear and I was going to have to try and give Mitchell back his life. He needed my forgiveness and I still wasn't sure if I could give it to him. I was at least willing to try.

Chapter 3

It didn't take much to plead our case with the Deacon. He had all, but given up on the fact that we were going to keep our noses out the business of others. He was still a little taken aback by our willingness to walk back into the thick of things.

I'm not going to try to stop you, but I'm not going to send anybody else with you on this insane mission of yours. If I did, then I would be just as culpable as the both of you for their safety. At least this way, I'll be able to sleep at night and be able to look at myself in the mirror in the morning and know that I did everything I could to protect my people. You two are the exception to the rule. Sometimes I think that you take too much on. That weight is going to wear you down, until it pushes you into the ground."

Jacob and I need to do this. You may not think it's necessary, but Mitchell is my responsibility. I shied away from my Amish background for a place of hatred and vengeance. Those days are over. I'm not going to put Mitchell through any more hell than he's already been through." It didn't look like the Deacon was listening, but I could see in his eyes that he was visibly impressed that we would do something like this.

Jacob had already packed some stuff, but not nearly enough for what we would need for this trip. We had what we could carry and we haggled with a nearby farmer to use his truck, as a means of conveyance to get back to the village in question.

At first he was hesitant and I didn't think that he was going to back down, but then money changed hands. Even though I believe that wealth was the root of all the evil, didn't mean that it didn't come into play once in awhile.

We bounced around on the road feeling like our kidneys were going to come out of our mouths. We were listening to the cackle of chickens in the cages that were back here the entire time that we were taking the ride of our lives. Jacob held me close and we pretended that we were in the countryside and enjoying a day together. For this moment we were not in the decimated land of Haiti. It gave us a moment of solitude. Even though the smell of the chickens was a little bit hard to take, didn't mean that we were not going to be able to stomach it.

It was about a few hours later that we finally arrived. The farmer didn't even stop and make any sort of small talk. He turned right around and drove out with puffs of blue smoke coming from the exhaust. We stood there on the dusty road, watching him recede into the cloud that he was forming behind him. We then turned and looked at the place that had started all of this. Mitchell had taken us and everybody else that he found on the bus. From there, it was a short trip to a hell that he could never even imagine. He was only trying to do what was right for his people. Now he had lost himself and was trying to find himself at the bottom of a bottle.

It didn't take all that much to find him and we just followed the raucous laughter and the clinking of glasses. We walked into this bar with him sitting there regaling people with stories of his past Glory.

Do you people know that I am a hero? I was the one that got rid of El Diablo and I was celebrated for that. Now you look down on me like you are better than me. I made it possible for all of you to walk out on your streets and live your lives, You don't worry that El Diablo's men will come by and collect what you worked, so hard for. You should all be bowing down at my feet and worshiping me as a God. Instead, you sicken me. I don't even know why I bothered to put my life on the line for the likes of all of you." He was waving the bottle around and then his eyes came in contact with my own. At first he didn't understand, then there was a moment of recognition. A flicker of something and then his face hardened.

I hope that you're ready for this, Bethany. He really doesn't look that happy to see you." Jacob was my guiding light and without him standing by my side, I'm not sure if I could have faced Mitchell again.

Well, if it isn't the lady herself. I never thought that I would see your face again, Bethany. You have forsaken me, put me on notice and made me feel like I was worthless. The only way that I felt anything was by drinking. Do you know that the more you drink them more you become numb to the fact that you've become a monster?" Bet you didn't know that. You come into my life with your holier than thou sermons and then you walk out. Well who needs you? Not me and not any of this fine people."

Mitchell, it's good to see you again. Maybe you should put the bottle down so we can talk this out like civil human beings." He was still waving the bottle in front of the others. It didn't look like he was going to be able to form enough sentences for us to have that necessary conversation.

I don't want anything from you. I think that you should turn around and go back the same way you came. You're the one that made me believe that I was nothing,

I asked for your forgiveness and you spat in my face. I wanted you to understand and to give me the peace of mind to know that I did the right thing. You turned your back and then you left without even trying to lift me up into the light. You should be ashamed of yourself. I don't want anything to do with you." Holding the bottle, he walked by me and I could smell the liquor on his breath, as he went outside.

I told you that he wasn't going to be very receptive. Maybe you should rethink your approach. It's obvious that he's drunk and he's going to need the rest of the night to sober up. Maybe in the morning, you'll have better luck in reaching him." Jacob and I went to find some place to sleep and we didn't have a whole lot of money. Thankfully, a local that knew about our exploits and what we did for this village had decided to take pity on us. Speaking of pity, I looked around and those that were in the bar were not treating him like the hero. They were treating him like a pariah and instead of trying to help him; they were letting him find his way into the blackness that was slowly covering his soul.

Chapter 4

I slept for a little while, but I soon woke up in a start to realize that I couldn't give up that easily. I slipped out of the bed that I shared with my husband. I looked down at his form and I knew that he wouldn't like me going out on my own. It didn't matter, because I couldn't sleep. I needed to clear my head of the conscious thought of making Mitchell into who he had become. People perceived him as nothing. He was what they would wipe off the bottom of their shoe.

I put on my clothes buttoning up my dress all the way to my neck. I put on my bonnet and went out into the night. It was still early and I had a pretty good feeling that he would still be at the bar. After we left, he probably stumbled back and began to put them down one after the other.

I put the gun in his mouth and I pulled the trigger and I don't regret a damn thing. I'll have you know that I'm the one that gave you all of your lives back." I stood there at the doorway not quite believing that he was still sporting the same old phrases. It seemed unlikely that he would live in the past. It was the past that made him the man that he was right now. I saw the pain in his eyes and I went over and sat down beside him with his back turned towards me.

I'll take water." The bartender scoffed and then he went back to retrieve what I had asked for. What came was not water but some murky disgusting brau thing that wasn't fit for consumption.

I'm sorry lady, but water is not exactly the easiest thing to consume around here. If you want real fresh water, then there is a spring about 5 miles away. I think that you should rethink your decision to drink that." I pushed it aside and I almost lost it. I put my hand up to my mouth to simulate that I was going to give up the supper that I had in the company of the young family that we were now staying with.

Oh my God, isn't there any way that I can get rid of you." Apparently, he had noticed that I was there. I was now ready to address the elephant in the room. Haven't you done enough already? You can't continue to put yourself through this. You're obviously looking at me like I'm a lost cause. You're right, I can't be redeemed and there's no way for me to come back from what I did. I don't regret it, because it was necessary at the time. I would do it again. I can see that is not what you want to hear, but I can't help that. I had a job to do and my people were looking to me to do what was necessary and I did it."

You did that all on your own, Mitchell. I tried to stop you, but you weren't listening. There are other ways than violence and I thought that we taught you that. Maybe I was wrong. I do apologize for walking out. You obviously tried to appease your conscience by talking to me, but I didn't wanna hear it."

Bethany, you look down on me with moral judgment and you came here willingly to help, but you really don't know what we've gone through. This catastrophe brought us together, but also tore us apart. People were lost and they died and we have to live with that for the rest of our lives. For this El Diablo character to come in and try to capitalize on that loss was despicable. You're naïve and you are stupid if you to come here thinking that you could actually make a difference. It makes me sick to my stomach." He took another swig of the bottle and I could tell that it was not the same one that he was holding when we first arrived.

I don't think that there's any way to talk to you when you're like this, Mitchell. Maybe in the morning, we'll be able to discuss this, but not right now. You think that you're a hero and that people worship you. You can look around and you know that the dregs of society don't really care what you've done. People outside these doors see you and they really don't know what they can do to help. You could've gone to the priest to confess, but I don't think you've even done that. I don't know why I bother, but recent events have proven to me that my judgment has not always been sound." I got up, feeling this anger welling up inside and I just wanted to turn around and punch him in the nose.

Get out and don't come back. I don't need your help. This is where I'm supposed to be. For you to think otherwise only makes you look foolish. I told you before that I don't need you. If I have to say it again, then you won't like the way I say it." It was obvious that he was showing some kind of anger. He was seething and the liquor that was running through his veins was not helping matters any. It was time to make a strategic retreat. I shouldn't have come back in the middle of the night in the first place. It was ill conceived and I'm sure that I would hear it from Jacob when I told him about all of this.

Chapter 5

I told you that he was in no frame of mind to talk to you last night, Bethany and you didn't listen to me. I suppose I can understand. He has been on your mind lately. With everything that's happened to Jonathan, I should've realized that you wouldn't be able to sit still for very long. I'm just glad that he didn't hurt you, because I would've done I don't know what I would have done, but I don't think I would've been very happy about it." I had no secrets with my husband and I told him all the gory details of what he had said to me and what I had said in return.

I just had to do something. I didn't like the way I left it the first time that we met him in the bar. I guess it didn't go any better the second time around. I should have listened. He might be in a better frame of mind to discuss this in the morning." I don't know if I had slept at all last night. I was tossing and turning with images of Mitchell drinking from that bottle and the kind face of Gabrielle turning into some grotesque monster with a whip in hand.

This time, let me go with you. If you don't want me to talk to him, then I will stand to the sidelines and make sure that everything is simpatico." That was actually a pretty good idea. From the looks of those that were drinking in the bar last night, I could've been in some serious trouble. I did notice some leering glances, like they hadn't seen a woman in there in quite some time.

Fine, if you think that it's necessary." I had this excess energy and I had seen some of the locals running to burn it off, but I wasn't much of a jogger. I enjoyed making things with my hands. I spent the last hour starting a new quilt for my *shtamm*. I already had the basics done. It wouldn't be long before I was starting to depict a story of my time here. I was going to give this to my *dochtah*. When I got back, I would show her what kind of adventure I was on. Maybe this would show her that a woman just didn't have to have her place in the kitchen. They could branch out and become more than what others perceive them to be.

I think in the light of day that Mitchell might be willing to talk to you. Just go slow and don't make any sudden hand movements." I knew that he was teasing and that he was referring to Mitchell as some wild animal that had been out in the forest too long.

I'll be sure not to get my hand bitten off this time. I'll use kid gloves and talk in hushed tones, so that I don't scare him away."

He wasn't at the bar and I was thankful for that. He at least left there sometime last night. He most likely had to sleep it off and it wasn't until noon that I finally saw him emerge from within an old barn. He was shielding his eyes and looked like he was struggling to remain focused.

I thought that you were a dream and I guess I have some explaining to do. I remember everything I said to you last night and I meant every word. I just didn't mean to be, so harsh about it. You were only trying to help and I suppose I just didn't wanna hear it." His shirt was open and I had to avert my eyes. It was wrong for me to see him half undressed. He saw that I was uncomfortable and began to button up with a smirk on his face. I forgot that you are Amish and I apologize for my manners."

I know that you didn't mean anything by it, Mitchell, but words do hurt. I felt them like a knife in my chest. I deserved everything that you said. It's just that I was having a hard time hearing it. I came here in good faith and I wanted to show you that I can get past everything that we've gone through together. Don't mistake this for forgiveness, because I don't think I can ever do that. What you did was reprehensible, but in your mind you were doing the right thing." That was the best that he was going to get out of me. I was just hoping that it was enough of an olive branch that he would take it.

I can't hope for anything more than that, Bethany. You've obviously thought long and hard about this. It would be wrong of me not to at least listen to reason." We were walking and talking and before long we were actually smiling and laughing.

Mitchell, I've missed this and you don't know how much. We had a good thing. I'm glad that we finally patched things up. I forgot who I was and what the Bible teaches about turning the other cheek. I suppose in time I could forgive you, but I will never forget the look in your eyes, as you pulled the trigger. You didn't look like you were enjoying it. It looked to me like you were struggling. If I had fought a little bit harder, I might've been able to make you change your mind."

I'm afraid that that wouldn't have happened. I had a one track mind and I knew what had to be done. If I allowed him to live, he would have the possibility of escaping or getting off on some technicality. Justice had to be served. I don't like having blood on my hands. I never d. I'm glad that you were around. I'm sure that I would've done other things that would have made you cringe. You gave me hope that people could be trusted. You never wavered, until that day that I showed you what my true intentions were." It appeared that we had come to some sort of truce. It was unsettled and it could break like plastic against my fingers.

Chapter 6

I would say that from the looks of it that things are looking up. You weren't screaming and he wasn't pointing his finger at you in an accusing tone. That's progress." Jacob was watching the entire thing and I could feel his eyes on me the entire time.

I guess we just needed time to hash things out. It was the distance that made this possible. Unfortunately, it also meant that he found his way into the bottle and I'm going to have to address that at some point. Like with Nicholas, liquor is an addiction. Anything can be an addiction if you allow it to be. It could be drugs, alcohol, or any number of things. It just depends on if you're willing to listen. It also depends if you are willing to let that addiction go. I have been counseling others and I've found that my words of wisdom and the verses in the Bible have given them the strength to stop cold turkey.

Bethany, it's not easy for people to admit that they have a problem. We both know that our *schaffe* is never done. Even when we leave here, we'll find some other cause to get involved with. We can't do anything about how people think. We can guide them and show them the way, but it's up to them to follow the teachings."

Jacob, I know that you're right and I wish that I could follow my own advice." I knew that if I had been more caring and understanding then Mitchell wouldn't be in the position that he is in today. This whole thing has been a teaching experience for not only those that I have counseled, but for myself as well. I've seen a different part of myself and it scared me."

Bethany, being scared is a good thing and it means you're alive. It means that you are a survivor. We've seen how people have picked themselves up from nothing. They dusted themselves off. Instead of wallowing in their grief and destruction of their homes they continued to move forward. Everybody could take lessons from these people. Even as Amish, we tend to look inside ourselves and not toward others. We segregate ourselves from the world, when we should be embracing those changes. I'm not saying that we should jump on board with technology. We should at least show understanding to those that do."

I guess everybody has decisions to make. It's not up to us to force our beliefs on them. You're right and all we can do is show them the way and let them decide if God is their personal savior. It's the only way that this works. It's the only way that we can really make a difference." I hugged my husband and I felt the warmth of his body against mine and I was happy to have him in my life.

I'm gathering from what you've said that you have decided to stay and see this through with Mitchell. Like you said, you have not even addressed the issue about his drinking. He needs our help, whether he knows it or not, and he's going to get it. He deserves nothing, but our best and we've seen him at his worst. That is not a place that he should reside in." I had every reason to believe that Mitchell was on the road to being the hero that people believed him to be at the time. We just needed to break him free of the anchor that was holding him down.

I still think that there's a lot of schaffe to do with him. I don't think that I could live with myself if I just walked away. I know that you understand that and I believe that I'm in for a long hard battle. It's time we shine a light on his problem and make him see that it's not only hurting himself, but others as well."

I think that my ears have been burning. I can see the both of you talking and I get this funny feeling that it's about me. You really don't have to worry about me and you can leave and rest assured that you were finally heard." He was always quite astute and he was a leader among men. It was that leadership quality that allowed him to ask his men to put their lives on the line every day. Trust me, I know what I'm doing and maybe you should give me the benefit of the doubt." It was funny, but he didn't seem to be slurring his words and the headache that I had seen him fighting with earlier was no longer present.

You look remarkably well for somebody that tied one on last night. It's only been a couple of hours, since we talked and you look more refreshed than ever. I don't think I've ever seen anybody bounce back that quickly from a hangover. I don't have anything to compare it to. I've never been in that position." I turned to Jacob and he shook his head to give me the indication that he had not been in that position himself.

What can I tell you, I've got a remedy that has been passed down from generation to generation. You could call it the hair of the dog, but that's not really the right way to describe it." I wasn't sure how he could say that. Last night he was stumbling all over himself and yelling obscenities to me and anybody else that wanted to listen. I've got everything under control." For some reason, I believed him and that was a little disconcerting to say the least.

I think that you should really look in on yourself and see these demons that have been haunting you. Once you have done that, then you can stop drinking and trying to find the answers at the bottom of a bottle." He smiled, put his hand on my shoulder and then he turned with a skip in his step.

Chapter 7

Mitchell, we came here for a purpose and we were wondering if you heard of anyone called the angel of death." At the sound of the name, he stopped and turned, but we couldn't see what he was thinking. I need to know everything you know about her. We think that she might be Gabrielle."

Gabrielle Are you serious? I can't believe that. She seemed, so nice and sincere. What kind of proof do you have that it's her?" He looked a little taken back by this latest information. I don't mean to stomp all over your theory, but she just doesn't seem to be the type. The angel of death, as you put her is somebody that has been working with El Diablo for some time. The most that I could find out about her is that she really enjoys torturing and dominating her followers. She basically brainwashing them with constant fear of reprisal if they were to ever go against her in any way. I just can't believe that it would be Gabrielle. I suppose it does make sense. What doesn't make sense is the fact that she was injured, so severely by El Diablo. Her eyes were cut in two places."

Jacob and I have talked about that and we believe that
her injuries were self inflicted. She most likely did that
to herself to gain some kind of sympathy. She wanted
to be the wolf in the hen house. She was able to do that
by garnering our trust. We took her in and we cared for
her. She was probably laughing the whole time that we
were administering to her needs. If Gabrielle is this
angel of death, then she was responsible for burning
down the homes that we had built for these people."

Bethany, I heard about that. I'm sorry that you had to
see all of your good work go up in flames. I'm sure that
was kind of demoralizing. I'm guessing that you rallied
the troops and you found a way to persevere. You
always do and that is one of the things that I admire
about you." He was still a bit of a surprise and I thought
for sure that he was going to fall down in the morning.
He didn't do that and I was scrutinizing him with my
eyes and I think he knew it.

Mitchell, I was wondering if there was any way that
you could find out where she's hiding. I have the right
to have a face to face with her once and for all. Don't
talk me out of it, because she fooled me and that's not
an easy thing to do. She made me rethink my position
and how I was helping people. We are doing it with a
kind word without any kind of research or some kind a
way to find out if they were on the level."

He motioned for us to follow him out of earshot of everybody from town. "I've been undercover. What you see is not exactly what is real. I've been cultivating sources and making people think that I am a no good drunk. I'm not saying I don't have a problem. I have to put up the right appearance. The bartender is a friend of mine. He gives me a couple of stiff ones and then replaces it with orange juice or water to simulate some kind of liquor. I know that I should have told you this before, but I really have been working hard to get to the bottom of this."

What about last night? You can't say that you were undercover and still spew those words in my direction."

I could tell you that, but I'm not going to. There are times that I get carried away. Sometimes I drink a little bit too much. Last night was one of those times. It doesn't happen often, but it does happen. I shouldn't have been on your case like that, Bethany. You've been nothing but a friend and I betrayed your friendship by killing with impunity. I didn't care about the consequences."

I don't like that you talked to my wife like that last night and I would appreciate that you never do it again. Mitchell, we still consider you a friend. Coming to you like this has rekindled the feeling like we have come home. We left things in a bad way. It's good to see that you and Bethany have mended some fences." Jacob has been trying to make me see things from Mitchell's point of view. It wasn't easy and it took Jonathan and everything that he had gone through to make me realize that I was most likely wrong.

You do know that you've been putting yourself out there in a bad light. Those that thought you were a hero are now thinking of you, as nothing more than some derelict. I now understand why you didn't go to your priest. You weren't fighting any demons, or at least you didn't think you were. I'm sure that drinking those few times to excess has opened your eyes." Jacob had his arm around me and Mitchell looked like he really did have the weight of the world on his shoulders. Then again, he always did, but this was a little bit different.

I see things exactly the way they are supposed to be, Bethany. I know that there is a man that can probably shed some light on the angel of death. I've been working him for a few weeks and I think that I've gotten him to the point that he's willing to speak openly. Unfortunately, I don't think that he's one to listen to strangers. You're going to have to let me approach him and stay on the sidelines and listen in."

Chapter 8

I can't believe that you heard all of this from a boy. He must've been beside himself and its no wonder that he was reluctant to help Jonathan in his time of need. I don't even know why he would help him. That is something that is a testament to the both of you and your new son Frankie. I didn't congratulate you and I know that his well being was very important to you. I'm glad to see that his brash behavior wasn't enough to make you turn away."

He can a bit precocious, but he reminds me of my *dochtah*. They both have minds of their own and I just know that when they do meet they're going to get along famously. They might even butt heads a few times, but I wouldn't expect anything differently." It was nice to talk to him like he was my friend again, even though I still could never forget how he had killed that man in cold blood. I had to get past it and I think for the most part I did.

We went into the bar and we saw this grizzled old veteran sitting at one of the booths in the dark with a bottle of jack on table and a shot glass in front of him. Why he was trying to fool anybody was beyond me. He was essentially a drunk in the middle of the street with a paper bag, but at least that would have made more sense. He was just trying to make people believe that he didn't have a problem. At least, Mitchell had already said that he did have one and was willing to work on it with me.

Jacob and I sat at the booth right behind his and Mitchell slipped in and began to talk to him like they were old friends.

James, you are a sight for sore eyes and I could really use a drink. The bartender won't serve me anymore, because of what happened last night. I think I got a little opinionated and started to throw my weight around." I didn't hear anything in response, except for the bottle being pushed across the table towards Mitchell. Even though he did have a problem, he was going to have to take that drink in front of this man to cement his bond.

I heard Mitchell grunt and then slam the glass down on the table. That is exactly what I needed, James. Do you know that that woman that came to see me last night talked about the angel of death? As if there is such a thing. I mean really, an angel of death.

Mitchell, you shouldn't joke about those things and the angel of death. He spit onto the table. It might have been gross, but it did show his distaste for the woman herself. She's no angel. She is an abomination and she might seem sweet and innocent on the outside, but she's festering on the inside. There is boils living with in her and she has no compassion or any semblance of right and wrong. I used to work with her and you can imagine that is the reason why I'm drunk most of the time. I can't get those images out of my head. I have to drown myself, so that I don't have to think about it. The only time that I'm at peace is when I'm sleeping and that's only when I am, so drunk that I can't stand up anymore."

You can't be serious. The angel of death is a myth that has been passed down to families to scare little children into eating their vegetables. It's like El Diablo. Once you get him alone, he's nothing but a man. If this woman is, so dangerous, then somebody should do something about it. I've already done my part and El Diablo is no longer a threat."

I've heard about what you did and you gave a lot of us the courage to walk away after he died. It was not without risk and the angel of death always seems to find us eventually. I'm not one to cast stones, but she doesn't deserve to live. I'm no angel myself and I should burn for the things that I've done, but she takes it to a whole different level."

I appreciate that you've been through a lot, James. We've all had our demons sneak up on us and take us by the throat. I don't suppose you know where the angel of death is hiding. Maybe I can do something to make sure that she doesn't come after you in the middle of the night. I'm in no condition to do it myself obviously, but Devlin will be more than happy to strike against the heart of the woman herself."

Just as long as I don't have to see her, I will write down directions to her encampment. I can't be sure that she's still there, but she is a creature of habit and she likes things just so. If she can, she'll stay there, because she knows that she has control of her environment. Just leave me out of it. I really don't wanna talk about this anymore." It was apparently bringing up some bad memories. He was actually taking the bottle by the neck and guzzling it like it was water.

Mitchell got up and swayed on his feet, before grabbing onto the table for support. I wasn't sure if this was an act or he needed to do that after taking that one shot. He turned and smiled and basically told us that he we should give him a couple of minutes before following him out. We stayed there in the darkness. We heard a thump and then looked over to see that James had passed out with the bottle in his hand. He was sleeping on the table with his head turned to one side with drool coming out of his mouth.

We went out to find Mitchell standing there impatiently bouncing back and forth on each of his feet. I've looked at his directions and they're pretty clear-cut. We can't do this on our own. We don't know what kind of numbers we're going to be coming up against. We're going to need help and that means I'm going to have to reach out to the only person that I trust more than myself. Devlin knows all about my under cover stint and I think it's time that I come out of retirement."

I'm still going to be very surprised if it's Gabrielle. That's not going to stop me from taking her down. She can't be allowed to do that to children and this time she will be held accountable. This time, there is going to be a different outcome than El Diablo. I do hope that I have made myself perfectly clear, Mitchell."

I promise that I won't kill her, but when bullets are flying, there is virtually nothing that you can do to predict what's going to happen next."

Chapter 9

It's about time that you found something out, Mitchell. I've been worried about you. You know that you have a problem and being in close proximity of all of that alcohol had to be taking its toll. I'm glad that you found out this information about the angel of death. I have made arrangements for our men to join us on this expedition." Devlin was a dark skinned Haitian. There was compassion in his eyes, but there was also a strict moral code that he followed each and every day. The only reason why I knew that was because he was carrying his abible like a personal life line.

I guess I have my new friends to thank for the information. It doesn't hurt that James, somebody that hasn't been very trusting of anybody was willing to impart this wisdom on me. Don't worry about me, I'll get clean and it's just a matter of getting into the right mindset. I can't begin to tell you how hard it's been not to talk to you. I had to put on this air of someone that didn't care about life anymore. Even my friends have no idea and when they find out, I doubt that they're going to take it very kindly." Mitchell and Devlin were two sides of a different coin. I could see that Devlin liked to do things his own way. He followed the teachings of the *mann* himself. That was no more evident by the cross that was around his neck. He touched it absentmindedly every so often, most likely to remind himself that he was on the path of righteousness.

I hate to interject, but I think there is something that we have to discuss." They both turned to look at me and Jacob. We've given you this information freely and we expect you to use it in the right way. With that being said, Jacob and I will be going with you. Don't even give me that look, because I don't need it. I've been on a roller-coaster of emotions and hearing that Gabrielle is most likely this angel of death is not helping. I feel sick to my stomach, I'm queasy all the time and I just know that all of this is slowly making me ill. So, if either one of you have arguments about why we can't go with you, then I expect you to keep it to yourselves." My stomach was lurching and it had been that way for the last a couple of days.

My wife speaks for the both of us and if you don't agree to take us with you, then we will just go it alone. We know exactly where this encampment is. It might take us a little while to get there, but we will."

Mitchell you never told me that your friends were stubborn. I see that we're not going to get anywhere with them. I think that you've been down this road before. If you know of any way to get through to them that this is dangerous and that they shouldn't come, then by all means give it a shot."

Devlin, are you out of your mind? She has been an albatross around my neck from the moment I met her and I wouldn't have it any other way. She has kept me on the straight and narrow for the most part. The only time that she wasn't able to show me the error of my ways was when I had El Diablo right where I wanted him. Believe me, I don't regret that moment, but I do see his face all the time when I am asleep and even when I'm awake. It's the reason why I turned to the bottle and to an old friend that I thought was long dead and buried."

I understand and these two are the ones that have been talked about in reverence by the locals and by the priest. I don't think there's any way around this. We may as well just get it over with. I expect you to be responsible for them. They are your friends and not mine." He turned in his camouflage gear and began to fiddle with a few automatic weapons that were splayed out on the kitchen table. I heard the stomping of boots and then Mitchell's men came in ready to take the fight back to the streets.

Mitchell was the one that addressed them all. We'll leave half a dozen soldiers here and we'll take the rest and go deal with this matter." Being soldiers made them very well aware of the dangers. I've heard that there were others trying to fill the void in the vacuum left by El Diablo. It was small insurgents that were dealt with accordingly by Devlin and Mitchell's men. People were on notice that there was a new sheriff in town and if you crossed them, then you would have to face the consequences.

Chapter 10

We spent the night going over the details of how we were going to make our approach to the encampment. It wasn't going to be easy by any means and there could been foot soldiers keeping an eye on the place.

If everybody is agreeable, I think that we should all get some rest. It's going to be a very big day tomorrow." Mitchell was a good man and what he said had merit. Jacob and I found the same place to sleep, as we had done before with the family. We slept in each other's arms and listened to each other's heart beating, until finally the streaks of sunshine woke us up. We were a little worried that they had left without us. We dressed in a hurry and walked out with Jacob affixing his hat on top of his head. His beard was quite bushy and I enjoyed the way that he had become a man from the moment that I married him.

We found the others outside waiting and they were impatiently staring at us. We were wondering if we were going to have to come in there and get you. There was talk about leaving you behind." Mitchell had apparently convinced them that it was our right to confront Gabrielle after everything that she had put us through.

I took him aside and walked down and away from the others for a moment. I had something to give him and I wasn't sure if he would be receptive. It was something that he had lost a long time ago, but something that I had forgotten to give him back, until this very moment.

Mitchell, I know that you have been dealing with a lot and I promised to get you back on your feet. After all of this is done, I'm going to make sure that you get the help that you need to find sobriety all over again. In the meantime, I think that this belongs to you." I passed him the Bible and he stared at it for a moment. He took it and placed it against his chest.

I think you're right and I did lose this. I'm glad that you found it for me. I found myself struggling and even though I didn't have this with me at the time, I still felt a pull towards the church. I even went inside and sat down and talked to Him at length one night. I never expected him to answer, but then there was a flicker in the candlelight. It could've been just a breeze, or it could have been a sign from him that he was listening. I would rather think that he was listening. He has sent you back here to show me that I didn't have to continue down the same path." We hugged and I was glad that his faith was restored in humanity and in *Gott*. We were

141

going to need that steadfast belief to get through the next moments.

Mitchell, Gabrielle is still out there. We found you and we brought you back into the light. You can't go down that same rabbit hole again, or you're going to lose yourself for good. I think we both know that and I think that is the reason why I should be by your side for the rest of this journey. Trust in yourself, trust in *Gott* and I think that you'll find that he has always been watching out for you from the moment that you decided to kill El Diablo. Your forgiveness is at hand and the flicker of the candle was his way of telling you that he has always watched over you. When you thought that he wasn't, he was always there in your footsteps." This was a chapter in my life that I was happy to close. His salvation was giving me this inkling that everything was going to turn out the right way.

Never was that more clear than finding my friend and bringing back that trust that had been broken. It didn't matter what he did and from now on ad nauseam, I would be constantly in his ear. If I wasn't around, then the Bible would take over where I left off. I was sure that he would be okay. With my help and his faith, he would become the man that I remembered.

BOOK 12

Rachel H. Kester

Chapter 1

I saw the way that Devlin and Mitchell were together and it was like an explosive charge getting ready to go off. They were constantly at odds over what was the right course of action and now we had gotten to the meat of the problem. There was no denying that my hand was in there somewhere and that Mitchell was listening to me for a change. Jacob and I stood there and watched them bicker. I wasn't sure what to do to try to contain the situation.

"I don't get it and I don't know why we are arguing this point, Mitchell. She obviously needs to be dealt with permanently and I thought that we were on the same wavelength. I don't know what changed, but I don't like this spineless man that is standing in front of me." I could see that Devlin wanted the old Mitchell back, but he had changed for the better and I was hoping that it was going to stick.

Mitchell came up to Devlin and pulled a knife from out of nowhere. Her pressed it against his neck and looked him in the eye "I don't like the way that you're speaking to me and I might just have to cut out your tongue to make you realize just who is in charge around here." This was the old Mitchell raising his ugly head and I guess there would always be that part of him that wanted to use violence and intimidation.

"This is exactly the person that I've been looking for! Where was this fire? You need to get it back. If I get the chance to take her out, then I'm going to do it. Not even your Bible thumping friends are going to stand in my way. You really should know that they are bad influence on you and that you are losing that edge that you had found." Devlin wasn't even afraid. He was showing nothing, but contempt for the *mann* that had the knife pressed up against his throat.

"I think that we need to take a moment and breathe. We obviously have a difference of opinion, but that's healthy. I know that each of you have your own way. I know that this is not going to be very popular, but I do want her taken alive. She needs to face up for the crimes that she has committed to these people. I would like to give her time to atone for her sins and by going to jail; she'll have plenty of time to think about what she's done." I was hoping that Devlin would see the same thing that I did. Gabrielle or the angel of death did not deserve a quick and final end.

"This is not your concern, lady and I don't appreciate you filling my friends head with nonsense. These are the kind of things that are going to get him killed.

145

Without that edge, they're easy prey for anybody that wants to take them down. I have to be the voice that get's through to his thick skull. His people need him to be strong and decisive without hesitation or delay. He needs to be able to strike while the iron is hot and do what is necessary. If he can't, then somebody else, namely me, will step in and do it for him. If I have to do that, then he will lose all the respect that he has garnered, as a leader and it will be all your fault."

"I don't know how many times I have to tell you this, Devlin. I'm the one in charge. Just because I gave you the mantle of responsibility while I was undercover, didn't mean that I wanted the power to go to your head. Your ego is the size of a melon and if you're not careful, I'm going to have to split your skull open to make you realize it. For the time being, I'm going to go with Bethany's plan. We need her to stand up for what she did and for everybody to see her, as the monster that she is. This will give people closure. They'll be able to close that chapter in their lives."

"I still don't like it, but I can see your point. I still think that the best thing to do is to get rid of her, but maybe you're right and that people do need to see her. If we can bring her in alive, then we will be able to give these people some kind of peace of mind. I'm sorry that I got a little hotheaded, but sometimes you do rub me the wrong way, Mitchell. I don't know what it is. It might be that we're, so unlike that I find myself in competition for the respect of the men. Like your friend said, this is a difference of opinion. We need to have our head on straight going into this. If we don't, then we may as well just lie down here and die.

It was never my intention to put them at odds, but it was nice to see that my words of wisdom were getting through in the end. I was worried that I was going to have the same kind of problem, as the time that we went after EL Diablo. I couldn't make up my mind if the angel of death was worse. Either way she had to be stopped before she did any more harm to any more *kinner*.

"I'm trying to stay out of this, as much as possible, Bethany. It's very hard to stand here and listen to them talk to you like that. Devlin might think that killing is easy, but we both know that killing someone is never easy. Violence is never the answer, even though I have strayed from that path from time to time. As your husband, I want you to know that I will be there to make sure that they hold up their end of the bargain." That was all that I could hope for. I was glad that he could be the strong silent type.

Chapter 2

We were in a convoy of at least three other vehicles and Mitchell and Devlin were leading the way with Jacob and I holding court with them. We arrived at the encampment and we had made our way up to the top of the hill through the cover of darkness. It was very early in the morning and the light of the sun was just barely creeping along the skyline. I could see it and I knew that we needed to have the element of surprise on our side.

Jacob and I knelt on the ground with both Devlin and Mitchell. They were the perfect contrast to each other. Devlin was the strong black man of Haitian origin and Mitchell was the white counterpart with a mind of his own. If you were looking at them, you would think that Devlin would be the one that held all the power in the palm of his hand. That wasn't the case.

"I was right. I had a pretty good idea that they would have a sentry post nearby. I also see several others in the brush hiding from sight. We need to take them out, so that they can't alert the others to our location." Mitchell was using a pair of binoculars and he turned towards Devlin and I could see another fight beginning to form.

"I agree with you and it might be distasteful, but we have to sacrifice them for the good of the many. Send in Andrew and Taka. They are our best and we're going to need them to make it, as efficient and as quick as possible. We can't even allow them to get off a shout or utter a moan. Anything could ruin this for us and we can't allow that to happen." I was afraid that I was going to have to intervene. It appeared that both men were finally on the same page.

"I hate to interject, but I would implore you to use non violent methods. You can take them out, but just don't kill them." I could see that Devlin was not at all happy with me saying this out loud for everybody else to hear. "I don't mean to be disrespectful, but killing should never be easy. Life is the most important thing and if we lose sight of that, then we may as well hold our hands up and surrender. *Gott* gave us the right to choose and that was not a gift given lightly." I'd said my peace and I could only hope that they would see that it was the right way.

"If we don't kill them, then they have the possibility of waking up and becoming a threat. I understand your sentiment for life and I agree with you in theory. Unfortunately, there are always casualties of war. Trust me, if you don't think that this is war, then you have no idea what is happening here. Bethany, I'm going to state my case, as eloquently as possible. I don't want to die here and I'd rather they die. It might not be right, but they knew that consequences of their actions going into this. We all do and we all accept the fact that dying is a big possibility."

"Devlin is not wrong, but is not right either. I've learned through quiet contemplation that putting my hands around somebody's throat should never be without regret. I don't want to see that look in Andrew's and Taka's eyes. They've already killed enough. Their hands are stained with the blood of their victims. I would rather send Conner and Linus and they can find a happy medium. If we send Taka and Andrew, they will have no choice but to kill on sight. Let's give these men a chance to walk away and if not, then they will have to face the consequences."

"I don't know what it is, but hearing you speak, Mitchell and Bethany at the same time is almost too hard for me to push back. I don't know if it's because she is right, or the fact that you are following her without even questioning her motives. You probably don't think that she has any, but I've been around long enough to know that goodness comes at a price." I wasn't sure how I should take that. There was a semblance of truth. My true motive was that I didn't want Mitchell to get lost in the shuffle again. I didn't want him to go down that road where he wouldn't be able to find his way back.

"I don't think I'm asking for the world. I'm just trying to be fair for everybody. These people that you look at, as the enemy have families and friends that will miss them if they're gone. I don't want you to wake up in a cold sweat in the middle of the night feeling like you've killed your very soul. I don't want the blackness to envelop you and take you down into the abyss. If you see that as my true motive, then I'm guilty. I'll gladly stand and tell anybody that will listen that I just want to make sure that everybody is undamaged body and soul."

"I think that Mitchell and I can tell you, Devlin that Bethany does have a strong mind and moral fiber. She's never shown anything, but kindness to all those that have been in her presence with one exception. Even so, she has forgiven him. They have become fast friends. If that doesn't tell you what kind of person she is, then I don't know what will."

They called forth Andrew and Taka to keep an eye on things from right where they were positioned on the hill. They sent in Conner and Linus, who were a little surprised to see that their services were needed. They didn't question and they knew that their true purpose was to follow orders and to do what needed to be done.

Chapter 3

We all watched with bated breath, as they approached their targets. It was amazing to watch them at work. They were, so skillful that you barely knew what was happening, until the *man* that they were after disappeared into the foliage. I watched, as they squeezed the air out of their lungs by placing their arm over their throat and pulling them back. I was worried that one of them would get off an errant shot, but they didn't. They did their training proud and those that had been the target went down.

"I know that this might sound wrong, but I don't care. I'm watching this and it gives me a sense of pride to know that they're doing what's necessary. In its own way, it's beautiful, like art or some kind of painting that has come alive in front of our eyes." I had not seen that side of Devlin. I certainly didn't know that he had an eye for detail. He would probably be right at home in a museum of some sort. I would have gladly taken him around to show him some of the finer things. I did have to wonder if Mitchell and Devlin saw futures outside of being a soldier. If they did, then what would they want to do with their lives?

Mitchell had freely told me that he liked to write, but he only did it as a hobby. With all the experience underneath his belt, he could probably write a bestseller. Writing comes from the soul and by writing he might be able to expunge some of the sins that he has committed in the past. It would be almost cathartic for him to do so.

"I know what you mean, Devlin and it's like a dance that has two partners that move together so willingly." I didn't know if I saw it the way they did, but they were looking at it from a soldier's point of view. Clinical speaking, they were surgical and precise. They did not hesitate or show any kind of mercy. They didn't kill them, but they certainly weren't gentle in any regard.

"Jacob, I know that I shouldn't say this, but I don't think I like the way that this is going. They look like they're having way too much fun. You can see the smile on their faces, as they take down their enemy. That can't be healthy for anybody."

"I think that we should count ourselves lucky that they are abiding by the rules of engagement. We asked them not to use violence and for the most part they have done exactly, as we hoped they would. If it's me, I would be more worried about these two guys next to us. They have this killer instinct in their eyes. Each one is holding that trigger like they're just waiting for the opportunity to strike. One of them is licking their lips with impatience and the other one is staring down the barrel of the gun like it's an extension of himself." I looked at the two guys in question. They weren't exactly subtle about their intentions.

"Bethany, I know that you're worried about those two, but I wouldn't be. They know their place in the hierarchy and they understand that they can't just kill with impunity. They know that it comes from orders. They won't act without them. It's not in their DNA." I wasn't sure if I liked the fact that they could be, so easily manipulated. With one word from their leader, they would gladly fire off a shot that would take somebody's life.

"Mitchell, you'd think that would give me some kind of peace of mind, but it doesn't. It makes me feel sorry for them and for you. You are in a position where you can't even think without acting first. That has to be a little disconcerting to know that you are, so high strung that one pluck of your string and you would go off on anybody in your vicinity." We were given the sign by Conner and Linus that the coast was clear. We came down to join them on the outskirts of the encampment.

Pulling away the underbrush, Mitchell came face to face with an electric fence. This wasn't something that they weren't expecting and they were ready for it. Two guys came forward and placed these prongs on the fencing. We soon saw this spark. It meant that it was short circuited and that it was safe to cross over to the other side.

I was not about to put my life in my own hands. It didn't seem like I had too. Devlin was the first one to touch it without even giving it much thought. He could've been fried to a crisp and yet it didn't seem to occur to him.

"Damn, he just touched that like it meant absolutely nothing."

"I touched it because I had to. I couldn't let my leader do it. I certainly couldn't put the responsibility on any one of these men. This was my cross to bear and I did it. I don't feel any thing." He was now cutting the wire. I could hear the slight snaps, as the cutter forced its way through the meshing.

"Don't be so hard headed, Devlin and we both know that I would've done that if you didn't. We both have our peoples best interest at heart. You come off, as mean and hardened like a stone, but we both know the underneath you are just a big teddy bear. Perhaps, you would like me to tell them about your gardening." At the very sound of that word, he whirled around and glared at Mitchell. "Fine, your secret is safe with me… Mr. Green thumb."

"One of these days, you and I are going to come to blows, Mitchell. I'm not sure who will be left standing at the end of it, but you won't come out of it unscathed." They were making progress. They were giving us a small opening to climb through. It was getting close to the final confrontation. I was about to go through when I saw a young kid with camouflage standing there with a gun in his hand. He looked scared, but then his face changed. It looked like he had just made a decision. If I was to guess, I would say that he was thinking that capturing us and bringing us to the angel of death would garner him some brownie points.

The only thing I could think of was my *dochtah* Rebekah and my *shtamm*, including Jacob and the *mann* that I had married. I'm not talking about Jacob; my husband that had died was now prevalent in my mind. He would always have a special spot in my heart. It didn't matter that I moved on. H would always be there showing me through his guidance what was the right thing to do. They say that your life flashes before your eyes, but frankly it was more to the fact that I was looking to the future and seeing that it was never going to happen.

Chapter 4

The kid and I were staring into each other's eyes. I could see that tiny little *bobli* that he was when he was younger. That naïve young impressionable kid was in there somewhere. I just had to find a way to show him that his life didn't have to consist of suffering and death at every turn. I didn't know if he was going to listen, but I had nothing to lose and everything to gain.

"If you intend to do something, then I would advise caution. These guys have been conditioned and there's very little that they won't do for a kind word from whoever is pulling the strings. If you can't bring him around, then we will have no choice, but to silence him." I had a feeling that Taka and Andrew were around somewhere. They were probably in position and ready to show their might.

I looked past the kid and I saw that there were small outcroppings of buildings that had camouflage netting over top of each one. It was probably a way for them to stay hidden from the rest of the world, Courtesy of Mitchell getting the information from that old guy we now knew where they were.

It wasn't like I could answer Mitchell and my concentration was on reading this kid and seeing if he was willing to kill for his cause. His eyes told me that he was ready, but his trigger finger still hadn't gone all the way. There had to be something that was stopping him from taking that next step.

"Listen to me and if you do one thing in your life, then pay attention to these words. The angel of death does not deserve your loyalty. She has been an albatross around your neck and is taking you away from the people that love you." I saw him watching me, but so far his intent was clear. "You don't have to do this and it's very possible that El Diablo and the angel of death were responsible for your parents' death. They turned your innocence into a soldier when you should be eating ice cream cones and playing with your friends."

"She loves me. Nothing you say is going to convince me otherwise. If I bring you to her, I know that I will be given the honor of a higher ranking. She'll see me, as more than just a foot soldier, but somebody that is willing to do anything for her. I might even get the detail of protecting her myself." It was time to pull out the big guns and see if they were going to work.

"The angel of death has a lot to answer for. There is a time for everything. You must see it and you can't be that blind not to know that she is the cause for all of your problems. There had to be a time that you looked at her and knew that she wasn't your savior. She didn't bring you out of obscurity. She took your innocence and twisted it for her own purposes. Don't let her do that. It only gives her more power." I grabbed the Bible from Mitchell's bag. I placed it in front of me like my own personal shield. The gleaming cross on the front caused him to stare at it in disbelief.

"I don't want to look at that."

"You don't have to read it." I quoted scripture and his eyes lit up with recognition. There was no denying that he was religious. That was just one of the many things that the angel of death had taken away from him. "You obviously know what this says. It teaches you to follow the path that you were supposed to be on. You can't believe that this is that path. You might think that it is, but deep down your faith is still there ready for you to hold onto it for dear life. Show her that you can't be controlled. You might just get your life back." I saw a shadow behind him and I knew that it was just a matter of time before Andrew or Taka made their move.

He stood there and his hand began to shake. He began to mutter underneath his breath the Lord's prayer. It was like he was waking up from a bad dream. His gun lowered and then he placed it at his side where it was no threat to anybody. The shadow that I had seen disappeared.

He pulled the fencing open for us and then turned his back, so that he didn't have to witness the betrayal to the one person that he thought he could trust. He was fighting the conditioning and his own childhood at the same time. He was fighting the natural instinct to do the right thing or to keep following the word of somebody that he didn't owe anything to. I didn't try to touch him or say anything to make him change his mind.

"I feel sorry for him and I hope that he will find his way back to the light." Jacob was a wealth of information and I could see that he was visibly distressed over how the kid had been feeling. He wasn't the only one and I could see my *dochtah* in his eyes. Frankie could've easily walked on the same path. We had plucked him from a life of destitution and slavery. It made me feel good that we had thought of him, as somebody that could be saved.

When everybody was clear of the fence, I looked at the kid and saw that he was closing his eyes. He was trying to justify his actions and the best way to do that was to pretend that he hadn't let the enemy into camp. It was the only way that he could live with himself. I was not going to do anything to make him think otherwise.

Chapter 5

I wanted to turn around and take the kid into my arms and tell him that everything was going to be OK. I just didn't have the time to do that and maybe after this was all said and done I might. I was glad that I was able to make him see the truth, at least for a little while. I didn't know how long that was going to hold, but at least it was a long enough for us to get inside the fencing.

"I want everybody to fan out and find the angel of death. When you do, radio the other ones. Approaching her is not going to be easy. She has all of these kids underneath her thumb. Bethany may have been able to reach out to that one kid, but that's not going to work on all of them. It's obvious that she has a hold and they probably don't even realize that she has been responsible for everything that has happened to them." Mitchell was giving his speech and I looked around at his men and I knew just from looking in their eyes that they were paying attention intently.

"Our leader has spoken and we will not fail him. Failure is not an option and we all know how important this is. Don't make the mistake that she can be reasoned with. She can't. Don't kill her, but don't give her an inch or she will take a mile. This girl is dangerous, unpredictable and if you're not careful, you'll be the one that will have your name scrawled across the headstone." Mitchell's way of leadership was to encourage and Devlin's way was to put the fear of death into everyone. In a combination of the two, it was more than enough to get their men to follow their orders to the letter.

They all scattered like the wind and we stayed with Devlin and Mitchell. We made our way past couple of buildings and we heard people inside talking. I stopped momentarily to look through a window. I saw that *kinner* were being taught where to strike their enemy to do the most harm.

It was a clinical test and I had to shake my head in disbelief that this was really happening. "I don't know if I should go in there and stop this or not."

"You can go in and stop it after we have done what we came here to do. If you try to walk in there and preach, I don't think it's going to be met with favorable results. Bethany, trust me on this one that some of these kids are too far gone to give any thought their own safety. They will walk into fire for the angel of death. If you try to enter, they will act accordingly and become your worst enemy." I wasn't sure if I wanted to believe it, but the way that they were staring at the photo of the anatomy was a little unnerving. If I didn't know any better, I would say that they were ready to fight.

"I know that you're right, Mitchell, but that doesn't make it any easier to walk away." I took one last look, felt this pain of guilt and it was almost enough for me to turn around and crash the party.

As we rounded the next building, we heard a woman's voice. It was loud and I wasn't sure if it was Gabrielle or not. "You do as I tell you to do. You kill that man and do it before he kills you." She had her back towards us with her hands behind like a drill sergeant. She was wearing all green and her hair was tucked underneath this cap. "There is no crying in ranks. I don't like your attitude soldier. I'm not your mother and I'm certainly not your father and neither one of them are here to direct you. I'm here and you do as I tell you to or suffer the consequences." It boiled in my veins like venom. I did not like the way that he was being treated by a woman that should have known better.

"Keep it together, Bethany. We can't go in their half cocked. We need to do this by the numbers. We need to wait, until my people get in position to strike without them being the wiser. If we do this right, there will be no bloodshed and most of these kids will most likely lie down after the angel of death is placed into custody." I was more than willing to wait, but that changed.

"I don't know how many times I have to tell you this, so maybe I won't say anything at all." She reached to the side where I couldn't see. She pulled back this whip and brought it back. I stared incredulously, as she snapped it forward and hit this kid in the back of the neck. "If you're not careful, then I'm going to give you something to cry about." This was too much. There was no way that I could actually stand here and let her physically abuse these *kinner*. It was wrong and somebody had to do something before it was too late. The next time she pulled back the whip, I was practically on my feet and ready to dash out there and do something about it.

"Don't do it, Bethany and it's not worth it. We need to look at the end game and not get sidetracked because of emotions." Mitchell saw that I was reaching the end of my rope and then I shrugged him loose and walked out to face the woman one on one. I had nerves of steel, but inside I was shaking like a leaf. I saw her and she started to turn and when I saw her face, it was like I couldn't believe my own eyes.

Chapter 6

I probably should have given it more thought, but I just couldn't do that. There *kinner* were suffering because of my inaction. Seeing Gabrielle turn and face me was a revelation. I guess deep down, I was hoping that she wasn't the cause of all this.

"You will not touch those kids again, or you will face my full wrath. I was ready to throw the rest of the soldiers underneath the bus. I didn't, because this was my problem to deal with. If I were to mention them, then she would go on full alert. This way, she would think that I had come here alone or maybe along with Jacob. She knew that he was attached to my hip and as if on cue, he came out to join me.

"I see in your eyes that you're not very happy to see me, Bethany. You probably thought that you wouldn't be seeing me. I'm glad that I could shock you. It goes to show just what kind of soldier I am. I'm willing to do anything, even cutting myself. I knew that once you saw that I was injured that you would think of me, as a wounded bird. All I had to do was play up the angle of a young lady in distress. You think that my brother is the only one that holds any power in this regime. I was higher than he was. The reason why he was worried about me was because I did this to myself."

"He was concerned that you were taking things a little too far. He was the one that was always putting himself in danger and he didn't want you to do that as well. I can't believe that you are the same woman that I talked too openly about everything. I can't believe that you are the same woman that grieved your brother and then in your same breath, you disappeared from sight when we got back to camp. I know now that you were responsible for having our good work burn into the ground."

"I understand that you've been talking to Jonathan. Believe me; his day of reckoning is upon him. He should be dead by now and watching him die like that must've been horrible." This was my time to smile. That smirk on her face suddenly vanished.

"I guess you haven't heard. Jonathan is going to make a remarkable recovery. He was on death's door, but we were able to pull him back before he succumbed. You'd be amazed at how many folk remedies there are within the Haitian community. All we had to do was find a rare flower and then boil it down into a tea. You should see your face. You're practically out of your mind that he survived. We didn't find you because of him and that honor went to another. I'm not going to do him a disservice by telling you his name."

"I don't believe you, Jonathan should've been gone within 24 hours of the poisoning. No matter, he's a nuisance. Once I am done here, I'll personally see to this matter. Sometimes, you have to do things on your own if you expect them to get done the right way." I didn't want her to thank that I was careless, but if she believed that I was unarmed, then maybe she wouldn't do anything drastic. "I still can't believe you came here and you did it without any weapons. Even Jacob should have realized that my reach is long and my kids are ready to stand in front of me to take a bullet."

"They're not your kinner and you just finished telling them that you weren't their mother. You took them away from everything that they hold dear. You need to be held accountable for that. I still can't wrap my mind around the fact that you hurt yourself. One wrong move with that knife and you would have taken your eye completely out. You're just lucky that you were able to cause enough injury to make it look worse than it was."

"I don't get lucky, Bethany and what I did was exactly what I set out to do. I knew that once my love had died that I would have to take his place. That was already decided a long time ago. I do have to say that sitting beside you and listening to you prattle on about everything was absolutely priceless. I got a lot of information and I was able to use that against you. How do you suppose I got the location for your camp? I wouldn't know it was there, unless you took me right to the front door. I'm not talking literally and I already had everything in place, by the time that we arrived at your camp. I would've liked to stay around to see the look on your faces when you saw everything burned to the ground."

"I'm going to give you one chance, Gabrielle, if you don't take it, then I can't be responsible for what happens next." She motioned with her hands and then a contingent of tiny soldiers surrounded myself and Jacob. This was when Devlin and Mitchell made their presence known. It looked like we were in the middle of a Mexican standoff. It didn't look like anybody was going to budge. I would say that it was very possible that somebody was going to get an itchy trigger finger. Once the bullets began to fly, there would be no place to hide and no place to run.

Chapter 7

This didn't look good and the fact that we were fighting kids was not lost on either myself or Jacob. Even Devlin and Mitchell were looking around with their guns drawn and not sure how to deal with tiny kinner that really didn't know what the hell they were doing in the first place. They were under the assumption that they were soldiers, but they were only pretending. They might have thought that they were dangerous, but in the right light, you could see that they were ill equipped for the real thing.

That didn't stop them from keeping us in their line of sight and turning towards Gabrielle for some kind of direction. "Kill them…kill them now and don't leave any survivors." I saw that the kids were about to do exactly that, but I stepped in front of them and the soldiers. It might have been a stupid thing to do, but I could not just do nothing.

"I don't think any of you really want do this. Isn't there something inside of you that tells you that your place is playing and not fighting? You must see that this woman is the bane of your existence. She brings you nothing, but hardship. You can have a different life, all you have to do is lay down your arms and surrender. We promise that we will not hurt you." I was hoping that I wasn't just talking to hear myself speak. It was possible that my speech was lost in the conditioning inside their head.

I did have to pat myself on the back for reaching the one that we had found at the fence. For the most part, everybody had that inkling of good in them that they were hiding away for a rainy day. If I could coax that out of them, then maybe they would see that it was time to let the grownups deal with grownup manners.

"Don't listen to her, listen to me. I'm the one that will punish you severely for your disobedience." I saw her reaching for the whip. The look on the kids' faces told me that they didn't want any part of that. I grabbed it out of her hand. I raised it into the air and then held it like a trophy for everybody to see.

"Without this, she is nothing. Try and see through what she has been feeding you." Two older kids came forward and Mitchell and Devlin had no choice, but to use violence. They rendered them unconscious with the butt of their guns. It might've been painful, but it would've been a whole lot worse with a bullet in the back of the head. "Don't be like those two. They were too far gone and you're not. Your innocence is still there and you don't need this woman stripping it away and replacing it with anger and resentment."

The other soldiers arrived and they surrounded the angel of death and her conditioned warriors. If things went badly, then there would be casualties on both sides. Being in the middle, I'm sure that Jacob and I would have taken the brunt of the attack. There would be no way that we could survive and my *dochtah* Rebekah would grow up without a mother.

"I don't care what she says to you, do as you're told. Do it... Do it or there will be hell to pay." Without her whip, she didn't seem all that menacing. Her words were hollow and the kids were now looking for me for some kind of guidance.

"If you don't believe anything, then believe that your family loves you. Your parents might be dead at the angel of death's hand, but you can find some surviving relatives. You can have the life that you were meant to have. That only comes from seeing inside yourself. Look to your heart. If you can't trust that, then you can't trust anything." There had to be a part of them that was fighting back. I was sure that their head and their heart were telling them two different things.

The *kinner* did not have to be here. For the angel of death to use them like this was something that she should be ashamed of. Unfortunately, I knew that she wasn't. She was banking on their conditioning to bring her to victory.

"This woman is a trespasser and she is to be considered armed and dangerous. Get me out of here and whoever stands beside me will be rewarded handsomely." She was now bargaining, it was her own last ditch effort to regain control. There was no denying that there had to be a breaking point, but who was going to blink first was the question that everybody was probably asking themselves.

Nobody said anything and the silence was almost deafening. Something was going to happen and you could feel it in the air. The way the wind shifted was anybody's guess. I wanted to say something, but everything that had to be said was already said. It was up to the kids to decide which way they were going to land. I would say that they had a 50/50 chance of either way. It was too bad, because I was hoping for a lot more percentage, but I would take what I could get.

Chapter 8

If I couldn't reach the kids, then maybe I could reach the woman herself. If her last ditch effort was to control the kids, then my last ditch effort was going to be trying to make her see that this was wrong. I had been through a lot and I wasn't going to allow this one moment in time to turn me away from the face of *Gott.*

"Gabrielle, there must be something inside of you that tells you that you've already lost. Your brother is gone, your master El Diablo is gone and that leaves you to fight this battle alone. This has to be tiresome. Don't you just want to relax and stop all the fighting?" She stared at me and I felt the hatred coming off of her in waves. She really wanted to get her hands on me. The only thing that was preventing her was Mitchell and his men. She knew that if she tried to make a stand whatsoever that it would not be met with kindness.

"You can say that after what they did to my brother. You can stand there and look me in the eyes and still believe that everything is going to be okay? My brother died fighting a cause that he believed in. I had to stand there and watch. I had to make you believe that it didn't affect me and that his loss wasn't felt into my very soul.

The moment that he gave off his last breath was when the last piece of goodness died in me. You were responsible for all of this and had you not talked Mitchell into fighting back, then we wouldn't be having this discussion. El Diablo would still be alive, my brother would be still standing beside me and that is something that I can never forgive." It didn't look like I was going to make any headway.

"You have to see that what your brother did was of his own making. You can't possibly believe that I had any control over what happened. You were both wrong and for you to think otherwise only makes me look at you with pity." I knew that I had said the wrong thing. Her finger started to move the gun forward, when I heard that cocking of every gun in Mitchell's platoon getting ready to answer the call.

"You take one step closer to my wife and you'll find out that I'm not, as Bible thumping as you think I am. I've been known to get my hands dirty and your brother was the first one to push me beyond my limits. I wouldn't even dream of hitting a girl, but you are no girl. You are a monster in the world would be better off if you were dead."

"That may very well be true, Jacob, but as you can see I am still breathing. As long as I am, these kids will follow my orders. You may as well just put one between my eyes. That's the only way this is going to end. I may not be their mother, but they are my kids." The rest of the camp heard what was going on and piled out from every building in the area. It looked like we were in over our heads, but Mitchell soldiers were not one to back down from a fight. That took exception to those that were about to pull the trigger. They did what had to be done, knocking them unconscious and then tying them with zip ties.

"There's no way that you can run from this, Bethany. My kids are everywhere and I was able to get one of my kids into your camp to poison Jonathan. Once he was done, he got out of there, as fast as possible and came back to report that he had accomplished his goal."

"I see that fighting you is a lost cause. You're never going to listen to a word I say. I would pull out the Bible, but I think that you would scoff at the very idea of religion. You probably have no faith and that is something that you're going to have to live with. I want to do the right thing and give you a chance. It's the last one you're going to get. If you don't put up any resistance, then we won't have to act with extreme force. Do yourself a favor and tell your kids to stand down. Don't think that you're going to get out of this firefight. There are two sharpshooters right now aiming for your head and if you try anything they will have no choice, but to take you out." I wasn't sure if I was speaking out of turn. I had a pretty good idea that Andrew and Taka were out there somewhere.

"You speak a good game, but I've yet to see any proof to your claim." As she took a step forward with the gun halfway up, a bullet rang out and barely missed her feet by a fraction of an inch.

"The next one will end you. I may regret that, but it might be necessary to put you in the ground." I didn't want to kill her, but she was being stubborn. She wanted to strike back, but she wanted her kids to do it for her. She was a coward and she wanted one of them to do her dirty work, so that she could steal herself away from the scene of the crime.

Chapter 9

"There's no reason for this to escalate any further, Gabrielle." I didn't want to use her moniker of angel of death, because it would have given her false hope. She needed to know that she was humanized. She was not this big bad wolf that everybody thought of her as. "Gabrielle, look around and it's not like you're going anywhere. Even if the bullets did fly, you would be the first casualty. Live to fight another day. It's possible that you'll get off with some kind of technicality. You could be free to spread your terror on the Haitian people again." I was hoping that by using reverse psychology that she would see that the best course of action was to lay down arms.

I heard a thumping and I turned to see that the kids had dropped their weapons and were being placed in confinement. They were herded off and moved to one of the buildings where two of Mitchell's then stood over it from the outside. The *kinner* were inside, probably wondering what they should do next. It was going to be a long road back from where they were sent, courtesy of Gabrielle. They would need guidance and understanding. I had a few people back at camp that I trusted to give them a new lease on life.

There was only one thing for her to do. Then she changed the rules by taking a knife out and placing it up against her own throat. Mitchell's men stood ready to do something, but I could see that they weren't all that concerned for her safety.

"You don't have to do this and there's no reason to be a martyr. Take this as a victory and then come back stronger than ever. You may not have the kids, but I don't think that's your only play. I'm sure that there are other soldiers that are loyal to the cause. They may be scattered to the wind, but you could find them and bring them back into the fold." She was eyeing me and then her hands start to moved with the blade cutting into her skin. "Don't do it; there's no reason for you to put yourself through the agony of bleeding out. You probably don't know this, but if you do cut your throat, it's possible that you will live." She didn't like the sound of that, so she started to move the blade over to her wrists.

I don't know what came over me, but I smacked it from her grip and it went sailing out of her reach. She started for it, but Mitchell's men stopped her dead in her tracks.

"You have denied me my kids and you have denied me my right to join my beloved. You should be ashamed of yourself, Bethany. You stand there and I'm sure that you feel that this is the end of the line. It's not like I believe a word you said. You don't want me to live to fight another day. You just want me to back down and be taken into custody. I'm not going to go willingly." It didn't matter, because she was beaten and the soldiers now seeing that she didn't have a weapon started to converge. "I will fight them tooth and nail. "I'll use whatever is at my disposal including my teeth. Trust me, my days might be numbered, but I can still do considerable damage." I thought for sure that I was going to have to watch, as they pummeled her into the ground into submission. It would be the only way to make sure that she didn't do what she said she was going to. If given the chance, she would rip out the throat of any one that came near her.

"The battle is over, but the war is far from done. I don't know where this is going to leave you. It could be that you spend your days in a dark hole somewhere. It could also be that one of your followers will come to rescue you. Hold on to that" I knew that if she had the chance that she would kill me, which was the reason why I was staying a few feet away.

I heard a crack of thunder and then I turn to see that Gabrielle was laughing hysterically. She stared at me for some time and then she fell forward, until her knees planted themselves into the ground. Her eyes showed that the life inside was dying and then she pitched forward and fell on her face. Beside her was the knife not more than 5 feet away from her fingers. Behind her was the smoking gun of the kid that we had met at the fence. He looked around at everybody pointing their guns at him. He dropped his and came into my arms.

"I'm so sorry." He was completely beside himself. He began to sob into my dress. His tears were warm against my skin. I could see that he was ashamed by his actions. I just hoped that this wasn't the start of a downward slope for this poor innocent little one. The soldiers saw that the threat had been eliminated and that a child had done it. I guess my little speech to him about her being responsible for his parents' death had made an impression on him.

I held him against my body and hid him from the rest of the world. As I was doing this, the soldiers were now gathering the kinner and placing them into a truck to take back to camp. From there, they would be given counseling and maybe since they were so young, they would be able to come back from this. If Frankie could, then I'm sure that they could.

Chapter 10

"Mitchell, I don't like how this ended. I really want her to be accountable for what she did. That kid is going to need some major therapy. I've already done what I can to get him the help that he deserves. There are a couple of psychologists on this land. I have referred to him to them and they have taken his case seriously."

I was standing at the Airport with my bags packed and Frankie over by the counter reading a comic book. Jacob was sitting there in one of the chairs and reading a magazine. Our plane was about to take off and we were finally going home. We tried this already once with no success.

"Bethany, I guess we can only control what we can. Everything else is up in the air and her fate was already sealed from the moment that she decided to use kids in her war. Don't feel sorry for her. Fate is a fickle mistress that tends to get what it wants." Mitchell was trying to make me feel better, but the only thing that was going to make me feel anything at all was having my hand in my *dochtah's*. Her smiling face and joyful innocence would ground me once again.

"I guess I'm not going to miss you Mitchell. I'm glad to see that you have finally unshackled yourself from being a soldier." He had decided to come with us and we were going to give him a home and a place to write his masterpiece. We would be his muse and he would call upon us for inspiration. He would also have a very simpler way of life. He would find strength in those around him in the Amish community.

We all gathered together and I took Frankie's hand, only to see that he was looking at me like I was crazy. I decided to give him a little freedom, but still kept my eye on him. He had changed and he was actually looking forward to hard *schaffe* on a farm. I had to wonder what he would think when he saw cows and horses.

"Bethany, life is going to be a lot different without the constant threat of somebody trying to take what we hold dear. You and I are both going to have to get used to the fact that people don't need us, as much as they do here. I know what you said and I believe that soon we will come back. There's still a lot to do and I'm glad to see that your organization is staying to fight the good fight. Devlin will keep an eye on things and if anything happens that I need to know about, he will reach out." I hoped that this would be the end of their problems and to see them with hope was what was carrying me the rest of the way.

"Mitchell, I'm glad to see that you're coming with us. You need this time to collect your thoughts and put them down on paper. I've no doubt that this will be on the New York's best seller list. I understand that we will have a part in it and that you will use us and give us a chance to tell you our story along with your own. With everything that happened, I'm sure that the public would want to get our recollection. That's very important to me and I know that it is for you too. This will give you a chance to breathe again. On those nights that it's quiet, take it in and hold it close to your heart."

We went down the aisle. I sat down and I looked at Jacob and I think we were both thinking the same thing. We'd been here before and we literally held our breath, as the pilot came over the speaker. The stewardess told us the prerequisite fire drill or crash landing process. We were waiting, and when that new calamity didn't occur, we breathed a sigh of relief.

"I still don't know what to call you and for the time being I'm going to stick with Jacob and Bethany. It just doesn't seem right to call you mother and father. Maybe in time, but not right now." This was something that I could understand and Frankie was not one to dismiss those that had brought him up in this world. He might have known that they were gone, but he didn't have to forget about them. I would do everything in my power to keep their memory alive and in his heart for the rest of his life. He turned back to his seat and it gave me a moment of contemplation. It was time to tell Jacob and I'd been holding onto the secret for a few days. Had I told him before, I doubt that he would have allowed me to go with them on the expedition to find Gabrielle.

"Jacob, I have something to tell you. You're going to be a *daett*." He saw me rubbing my stomach. He placed his hand on top of mine and our *shtamm* was just going to get a little bit bigger.

Amish Crossroads Series

END OF THIS SERIES

Made in the USA
San Bernardino, CA
12 February 2016